Where Bluebirds Fly

Wendy Storer

To Phoebe,
(A little extra because
you deserve it.)
With love and
best wishes
. Wendy Storer
xxx

Published in 2013 by Applecore Books
www.applecorebooks.co.uk

Printed in Great Britain by Lightning Source
ISBN 978-0-9574812-7-5

For Mum and Dad

with love x

Chapter 1

When they first told me about High Fell Hall they called it a SPECIAL school.

I said, "I'm not a retard."

So they said, "It's a school for children with emotional difficulties."

And I said, "Then why are you sending me there?"

I was still in hospital, in one of the side rooms. They all stood around my bed and talked about me as if I didn't exist. There was Mum, my social worker Helen, my named nurse Siobhan, 'Hairy' Hickory my form teacher, Mrs Stein who is the TOP person at High Fell, and Mr Gillespie the psychiatrist. Gillespie was the only one who didn't speak; he just stood there with his arms half folded, stroking his chin.

Mum kept trying to hold my hand, except I wouldn't let her.

And Helen was all, "Please say something, Ruby."

But I kept my mouth shut and my thoughts to myself.

"High Fell is an option, that's all," said Helen. "That's why Mrs Stein is here; to tell you how it works and to help us make the right decision."

Help THEM make the right decision. I wanted to go home, but it was six against one and I didn't stand a chance. I tuned out. Made up a song in my head about lions and tigers and bears. And it worked until someone said something wordy and stupid and I couldn't block it out.

"The breakdown of family relationships …
obsessional behaviour … difficulties attending
mainstream school …" Blah blah blah.

After the last one I said, "What difficulty? I go,
don't I?"

Hickory said, "Your attendance is not the problem,
Ruby. It's your behaviour when you are in school."

He was talking about THAT drama lesson. The one
where we had to devise a piece about a social issue. I
wanted to do homelessness. I was going to be a girl lost
in a storm with her little dog, who meets a whole bunch
of whacky characters on the road to a happy ending. It
would have been fun. But my group chose domestic
violence.

Domestic violence!

They wanted me to act drunk. I said, 'Just because
you're drunk, doesn't mean you're violent.'

And Isaac Thomas said, "Yeah, well you should
know."

And I said, "What does that mean?"

But Isaac burst out laughing and no one else had an
answer. No one actually came out and accused my dad
of being a drunk, but that's what they meant. Anyway, I
wouldn't do it. It wasn't proper acting and they were
picking on me, so I lost my temper and walked out.

"One incident?" I said.

"Which incident?" said Hickory.

And Helen said, "You've walked out of a number of
lessons, Ruby. You seldom produce any written work
and you've been increasingly withdrawn. 'Closed off'
is how several teachers describe you. Everyone is
worried about you. And we know things at home have
been…"

I put my fingers in my ears, said, "Blah blah blah,"
and pretended I couldn't hear.

Mum shook her head. Gillespie raised his eyebrows. And Helen carried on talking. But I didn't want to remember how things had been at home. It wasn't until Mrs Stein started saying about the beautiful green countryside and the wildlife and the garden that I took my fingers out of my ears.

"…the perfect place for you to get better. High Fell Hall isn't like a school at all," she said.

As far as the last bit is concerned, they were right.

Chapter 2

It was late when we arrived and I was tired. I wanted to crawl into a bed, close my eyes to the world and forget I was alive. But Lily (the head of care) came out to meet us and Helen was pulling my bags from the boot before I'd even undone my seat belt.

"Be friendly," she whispered. "And smile."

Faces appeared at the windows. Nosy staring faces, looking at me. One of them was covered in face paint; white skin, green eyes, black lips, and crude zigzags over her cheeks.

I put my backpack on while Lily and Helen talked. And then I waited, wishing I could be somewhere else, away from prying eyes. But this niggly voice in my brain kept saying, "Be yourself, be friendly, be yourself…" and so like a total loser, I looked back at the faces and waved. Not a massive arms flying all over the place wave; just a tiny shake of the hand. Enough to make the painted one scream with laughter and the others join in. Even though the windows were shut, I could still hear them.

"Hole in the ground, please open up and swallow me," I said.

Lily stopped talking to Helen and looked at me, then the house. "Would you like to meet the girls?" she said.

There were five of them. Pearl, Bianca and Scarlet were about my age. Amy and Rachel were younger. Pearl was the one in weird make-up. But not only that; she was dressed in black from head to toe, including clunky boots and a leather glove on one hand. Amy wore pink fairy wings and a princess tiara. The others looked normal.

"Is this a fancy dress party?" I said.

Pearl, Bianca and Scarlet all snorted. I went bright red. Lily told them to be nice and to remember what it felt like to be new, and Pearl said, "Shall I show her THE ROOM?"

Lily said, "That's really kind, Pearl. Thank you." And to me she said, "Take a few minutes to unpack and settle in, then come down and we'll have supper."

When we got to THE ROOM I realised she meant MY ROOM. I wanted to be alone, except that Pearl was all, "Where do you come from? What've you done? Was that your social worker? Who do you live with?" She plonked herself on the bed and pulled my case towards her, clicking open the catches and lifting the lid before I could stop her. "Got anything to eat? Can I have a look in here…?"

"Leave it," I said, shoving the top down on her gloved hand.

Pearl tugged it free. "Suit yourself. Only trying to be helpful." She folded her arms, and looked all hurt.

"I'm sorry," I said. "It's been a long day." I took my backpack off and sat down too. The bed had a flowery pink duvet and white pillow cases. There was a white chest of drawers with pink handles, and an old wooden wardrobe and long mirror. The walls were white too, and looked wonderfully bare.

"I'm across the hall. Bathroom's next to me," Pearl said, arms still folded. "And you're not allowed in anyone else's room without permission, but they'll tell you that."

She so obviously wasn't going to go.

"I need the loo," I said, "I'll be down in a minute," hoping she would take the hint.

But she pulled open my door and leaned round it, pointing. "That one," she said, staying very firmly put. I didn't want to leave her in my room alone, but what else could I do?

In the bathroom, I sat on the toilet with the seat down and my pants up. I breathed a big deep breath in, then blew it out again; like I was blowing away all the noise and bad stuff. I closed my eyes. My head was spinning. I imagined I was in a whirlwind, a twister, watching my life whiz round and round. Helen. Mum. Hospital. Dad, drunk and falling over himself. Nanna ordering me to bed… and then there was Lucy, my baby sister.

"Oh, Lucy, I'm so so sorry," I said, out loud. The rainbow song started leaking out of my brain, through my mouth. Not like I was singing, more just humming with words. And I lost myself for a few seconds, maybe a minute.

When I heard noises outside the door, I dried my eyes on toilet roll, flushed the loo and washed my hands. "I have to get out of this place." If I was ever going to see Lucy again, I had to make it work.

Dear Lucy,

I'm going to tell you all about Nanna.

I want you to know everything. From the summer green tomatoes ripening on her windowsill, to the little red robin she fed in the winter. I want you to know how holding her hand was the safest feeling in the world and how stretching your arms around her middle, landed your head on her soft pillow belly. I want you to know that she smelled of freesias, strawberry cup cakes, and sometimes when she'd been gardening all day she smelled of fresh air; how her laugh was more of a funny giggle, how she would cry when she was happy and count to ten when she was mad, and how she always always always knew exactly the right thing to say or do to make you feel better.

I miss Nanna. And I miss you. I don't know how long I'll be here, but when I get out, I am going to be the best sister in the world. And that's a promise.

Love you,
Ruby x

Chapter 3

I didn't sleep. Well, not much. It took forever to close my eyes and in the morning, birds woke me. I pushed the flowery duvet onto the floor and went to the window, opening it as wide as it would go. In my own house you can't hear the birds singing because of traffic, but when I stayed over at Nanna's, every day started with wood pigeons cooing on the roof and a chorus of sparrows and starlings in the trees.

I thought of Nanna then.

A shiver went down my back and a picture flashed into my brain. It was Nanna, her eyes open and staring, a bright red halo round her head and her face ghostly white. My eyes pricked and I felt a lump in my throat. Missing Nanna was a physical thing.

"Get a grip, Ruby," I said. "The past is the past."

I made my bed, got dressed and went to the bathroom where I brushed my teeth and washed my face. Sometimes, when I looked in a mirror, all I could see was Dad. Today was one of those days on account of the bed-head and the big black bags under my blue eyes; the morning after the night before.

"I hate you," I said, then spat at the mirror. When I turned round, Pearl was standing in the doorway watching.

"Don't mind me," she said. "You go ahead and hate your face."

"I wasn't talking to myself, if that's what you think."

"No?" said Pearl, looking around the bathroom and double checking behind the door. She shrugged.

At least I wasn't wearing day old make-up. I pushed past her to go back to my room.

As I closed the door, she said, "Freak."

After breakfast, Lily sent the others off to their rooms, but kept me back. She wanted to tell me about the school set up, to walk me around the building so I knew where everything was, and give me an opportunity to ask questions.

The only question from me was, "When can I see Lucy?"

But Lily said she couldn't answer that one yet.

She showed me the comfy room where the telly was, the kitchen, the staff rooms, the main office, the school rooms, the big room where they did dance and drama and stuff like that. She showed me the art room, the therapy annex and the rabbit hutch. And then she said, "So, what do you think?"

What I thought was, I don't do art, I don't need therapy and I don't like animals. But Nanna used to say, concentrate on the good things, so I said, "I like drama."

"Drama?" said Lily. "Super! I shall remember that."

I don't know why, but it made me feel all sort of nice and warm and listened to. And for just a second I actually thought I might like being at High Fell after all. But then in practically the same moment, I glanced up and saw a figure at my window.

Pearl.

In my room.

I ran into the house, down the hall and up the stairs two at a time, shoving my bedroom door hard, hoping

13

to catch the sneaky witch red-handed. The door bashed against my bed, but the room was empty.

Lily came panting up the stairs behind me. "What's going on?" she wheezed.

"Someone was in my room," I said. "Pearl."

Lily frowned. "Are you sure?"

"I saw her, from the garden." No mistake.

I checked in my wardrobe, my drawers, and my case. Everything was neat and tidy, just as I'd left it.

Then Pearl appeared at the door with Bianca.

Lily said, "Have you been in Ruby's room?"

"Who? Me?" said Pearl, acting all innocent and surprised.

Everyone looked in my direction then.

"Could you have been mistaken?" said Lily.

Pearl was definitely in my room, but I couldn't prove it, and Bianca was holding onto her arm, like girls do when they're best friends. Their word against mine. "Maybe," I said, and then added, "I must be seeing things," to try and make a joke of it.

"Ah well, probably just a shadow," said Lily. "No harm done."

She went downstairs, leaving Pearl and Bianca still standing in my doorway.

Pearl said, "Talking to yourself *and* seeing things? They'll lock you up. Weirdo."

I closed my door and leaned against it. They weren't the first girls who didn't want to be friends with me. I was always the odd one out - the one without a best friend - but I stopped caring when Lucy was born. Friends could come and go, but sisters stayed with you forever. I kicked the door with my heel, and heard Pearl and Bianca laugh.

When I knew they had gone, I sat down on the floor next to my backpack.

Inside, were stones of all shapes and sizes, collected from all sorts of places. Each one was a memory. I tipped them out and started to put them in a line, darkest to lightest, recalling each and every moment they came into my life. I had lumps of granite, slate, limestone, and rocks I didn't know the names of; all collected from days out, school trips, and special events.

When I got to a tiny lump of chalkstone, I stopped. My heart beat faster and I froze for a second or more with it in my hand…

We didn't have family outings very often, so the chalkstone day was special. We went to the Downs. Mum made a picnic and Dad brought champagne to drink. I wore my dress with bluebells on. We flew a kite and Dad gave me a piggy back. We found the chalkstone together; me and Dad. And Dad used it to write 'I love Ruby' on a big rock.

…But now there were pen marks across the rough surface. When I looked closer, I realised it was a word, in jagged, almost impossible to read writing.

'Skitzo.'

So she had been in my room. I knew it.

I took the chalkstone into the bathroom and tried to wash it, scrubbing the ink with a nail brush. It wouldn't budge. I tried soap, and shampoo, and even toothpaste, rubbing as hard as I could, but that word just stayed there. And I could hear Pearl's voice in my head, saying "Skitzo, Freak, Weirdo."

It wasn't just a stone she had spoiled; it was a memory. I looked at the door and whispered, "I'll get you back for this."

Chapter 4

In the afternoon there was a trip to the farmers' market. Lily said there would be delicious double chocolate ice-creams, home-cooked cakes and buns to sample. Believe me I was tempted, but spending time with Miss Popular and her hangers-on was more than I could stand. I faked a headache and Lily took pity on me. Said I could borrow the portable DVD player and watch a film in my room instead.

When the mini-bus was out of sight, I crossed the hall and stood in front of Pearl's door. A sign, stuck on with sellotape, said, 'DO NOT ENTER – OR ELSE' in black gothicky letters dripping with red felt-tip blood. I went in anyway.

The curtains were shut and it took me a few seconds to get used to the dark. When I did, I saw heaps of clothes and rubbish on the floor and a chest of drawers covered in eye shadow pallets, brushes, bottles of concealer, foundation, mascara, and more make-up than anyone could need in a lifetime.

Pearl's black painted walls were studded with dozens of photos, and I picked my way through the debris for a closer look. "Huge family," I said, scanning pictures. An eyebrow pencil would have made easy work of revenge; a beard on one face, a pair of fangs on another or a dagger plunged into some innocent's head. But photos could easily be replaced. It wasn't proper payback. So I carried on looking for inspiration in the overflowing drawers, the wardrobe and under the bed.

Nothing grabbed me. Nothing screamed PICK ME at the top of its voice. Nothing that is, until the PINK BOX. And even then it wasn't so much a scream as a whimper.

The box was covered in dust and sticky sweet wrappers, and lay next to a rusty old biscuit tin. It certainly wasn't a thirteen-year-old's thing; more the sort of yuckified rubbish you had when you were seven. Pink love-heart paper peeled away at the edges and the pretend gold padlock hung off, broken. It was so out of place in all that gothicky black, I knew it must have sentimental value.

That's why she kept it. And that's why I took it. I didn't have a plan; didn't know what I would do with my treasure. I just knew it had power.

Chapter 5

Back in my room, I opened the pink box. Pieces of photo stared back at me. Not whole photos, like the ones on the wall. PIECES. People, cut up. A face here, a body there, an arm, a leg, or just an eye. Totally sick.

Some of the bits joined together. One of the fragments had a baby face on it. I found four other parts of the same baby and ended up with a complete picture; a mum with the baby on her lap. The mum was smiling. The baby was freakishly like photos of me at that age; maybe even a little bit like Lucy.

"All babies look the same," my dad said, once. It was my fourth birthday, the only birthday he didn't miss. Mum, Nanna and I went shopping at Bluewater, choosing curtains and bedding for my new bedroom. Dad stayed home and painted the walls. While we were out, we met a woman in the play area with a little girl who looked just like me. We played together for a bit, and Mum and Nanna and the other woman couldn't get over how alike we were. When we got home they told Dad. That's when he said it. "All babies look the same." And Nanna said, "Yes, Ryan, but Ruby's not a baby. She's four."

I hid the pink box in my wardrobe and went downstairs.

Alison, one of the care staff, was washing dishes in the kitchen. I picked up a tea towel and started drying.

"Are you okay?" she said.

It was never a good idea to remember the past, and I bet she knew I'd been crying.

When I didn't answer, she said, "Well it's lovely of you to help."

I shrugged. It's only what I was used to.

After drying up, I found the vacuum and gave the comfy room a once over, then stood all the books on the bookshelf next to each other with their spines facing out, in alphabetical order of author.

When the others returned, Alison made a point of telling them how I'd done chores without even being asked.

Pearl said, "Spare us from the neat freak," and Bianca thought she was funny.

After tea, Lily told everyone we would play some games. Ice-breakers, she called them. She wanted to give me a chance to get to know the others better, and vice versa.

"Everyone loves charades," she said. "It's just like acting."

We had to choose film titles or TV programmes and act them out so that the others could guess what it was. But I hadn't seen the films they'd seen or watched the same programmes on telly so I never guessed anything right. And they pretended they'd never even heard of my film - The Wizard of Oz - so it was all completely pointless, and I asked Lily if I could go to bed early.

I cleaned my teeth, changed into my pyjamas and folded my clothes, then slid into bed. I was definitely tired, but my head was buzzing with all the things which had happened that day and it was hard to relax. To stop my brain from thinking so loud, I concentrated on seeing the colours of the rainbow in the space behind my eyes. Red, orange, yellow, green, blue, indigo and violet. Red was easiest. My thoughts stopped racing, and my body began to rest. I felt dreamy and calm…

But then someone knocked at my door. I squeezed my eyelids tight, trying to summon the rainbow again. But Lily had a loud voice. I could hear her laying down the law about how many baby wipes anyone needed in one go. Bianca called her the Queen of Stinge and everyone laughed. There was another knock, my door opened and Lily whispered my name. Then I heard Amy and Rachel kicking off about hair straighteners.

"Nobody needs straight hair to sleep," said Lily.

And then suddenly - BANG! The door thwacked against the side of my bed and a tornado with fists whirled itself into my room and landed on top of me.

It hit my head.

I put my arms up for protection so it punched me in the back and ribs.

I tried to roll over, but its whole body was on top of me and I couldn't get free.

And it screamed, "Where's my box?"

Chapter 6

After they pulled her off me, Pearl just stood there panting, and shouting. "She's got my box! She's been in my room. I know it's her. Pleeeeease get it back…"

Tom and Alison stood in the doorway blocking the others, but nobody else said a thing until Pearl's gobby outburst ended.

Then Lily turned and looked at me. "Are you all right?"

"Yes," I said. "No thanks to her."

Pearl said, "Shame."

Lily fired a warning look, and then said to me, "What's this about?"

I shrugged.

Cue Pearl's rant. "She's been in my room and my pink box the one with the photos is missing and she's got it she must have it and she better not have damaged it or else…" Gasp for air. "I hate her."

Lily raised her eyebrows, and turned to me. "Have you been in Pearl's room? Did you take her box?"

"What box?" I said.

"You sad thieving cow," said Bianca, from out in the hallway.

"I want the truth, Missy," said Lily, talking to me.

I shrugged again.

"Then you won't mind if we search your room?" she said.

I did mind actually. I minded very much. But I stood to one side, folded my arms and said, "Do what you like." I knew they'd find what they were looking for. It didn't matter, because in a way I had already won.

They started on my chest of drawers, nosing through my underwear, my tee-shirts and my trousers; like they were public property. Lily looked under my pillow, ignored my book of Lucy letters, and then they started on the wardrobe. She pulled out my bag of stones, tipping them onto the floor.

Pearl said, "I told you she's insane."

When they searched under my shoes they found it.

Bianca and Scarlet pulled smug told-you-so faces, and Lily closed the door. "I want an explanation," she said to me.

"For the stones?" I said.

"Don't get funny with me, Missy. I meant an explanation for having Pearl's box in your wardrobe."

My face was hot and probably the colour of beetroot. The whole thing was beginning to annoy me. I should have told on Pearl for spoiling my chalkstone, but didn't because… well, what's the point?

And then Lily gave Pearl the box, which she grabbed with her gloved hand and held it right up close to her body, like a proper drama queen. She sneered at me; one of them lip-twisters you want to get hold of and bend just that little bit more. Lily opened the door and shooed Pearl out. She told me to stay in my room until morning when I would be able to DISCUSS the incident with Mrs Stein. And then she left.

Outside, Miss Popular was milking her moment to be in the spotlight, declaring that she would rather DIE than lose her precious memories.

When she finally gave up, I put my stones carefully away and wrapped my arms around my backpack for comfort. I tried to sleep, but it was never going to happen.

22

Dear Lucy,

When you couldn't sleep, you cried. If I heard you before Mum did, I would come and pick you out of your cot and sing you songs about rainbows, lollipops and happy little bluebirds. And I'd keep singing until you weren't crying any more, and then I'd stay with you till you fell asleep again.

Mum said that's what Nanna did with me.

I still see Nanna with my lids tight shut; silver hair and soft blue eyes, wrinkles like moonbeams. When I was little, I used to pretend she was the good witch of the north, sprinkling my dreams with magic dust. As long as Nanna was there, everything was all right.

Love you,

Ruby x

Chapter 7

The morning after the pink box situation I refused to go down to breakfast, so Lily brought it to me in my room. It was toast with jam, but only a couple of slices. I would have liked more and Lily said I was welcome to go and get more, but I didn't. The longer I kept myself to myself, the better it would be.

After I'd eaten, Lily waited for me to get dressed, then took me to see Mrs Stein.

Mrs Stein's office was a collection of wooden furniture; not nice clean grainy wood, like you get in home make-over programmes or weekend magazines, but death-watch beetle wood. Dark and fusty and infested with tiny holes.

"Ruby, you look extremely tired," she said. "Did you sleep at all?" Her head cocked slightly to one side like a puppy waiting for a treat. She pointed to a dead-brown sofa.

"Do you want me to sit on that?" I said.

She smiled. "I think you'd be more comfortable sitting down," she said. "And why not take that bag off your back?"

I held on to the straps, and sat down.

"This probably feels very strange to you," said Mrs Stein.

I shrugged and looked out of the window. It was a blue sky and a green landscape. There were hills, mountains, trees and fields as far as I could see. It was

24

beautiful, and totally STILL. Except for the birds. I hadn't realised just how lovely it was until then.

"The way we work here is different to a mainstream school. We're a home and a community as well as a school. We only take a few girls at a time so that we can really understand and help you as individuals..."

I was waiting for her to start the lecture about stealing and going into other people's rooms, but she went on to talk about respect and honesty and how the best way to make friends was to be open and trusting and I thought, that's rich, considering how I ended up in here…

It was Mum's night out with some people from work. Her first one since Lucy was born. I did her hair - nothing drastic, just soft pretty curls - and she bought a new dress. She joked, "Does my bum look big in this?" and kept fussing about it being right.

"You look lovely," I said.

"I'll be back by eleven," she said. "But don't wait up because I know you're tired."

Mum walked towards the gate, then stopped, turned round and walked back to the house. "I shouldn't go. It's not fair," she said. "I don't like leaving you. Why don't I just stay in and we can watch a film?"

She deserved a night out. "Please go," I said. "You know you want to."

"Are you sure?"

"I'm sure," I said. "Just have fun." That's what Nanna would have said too.

"If there's a problem, ANY problem at all, just phone me. Yes?"

"I promise."

"Eastern Tandoori, number by the telephone, just in case I've got no signal."

"Will you please go?"

I checked the doors were locked and all the windows were closed. I went round turning lights on, brought my duvet down and laid it out neatly on the sofa. I picked up The Wizard of Oz and slipped it into the DVD player. Even though it was ancient it was my bestest and most favouritest film of ALL TIME. It was the film Nanna and I always watched together. I sat down with the remote, snuggled into my duvet and was just about to press play when Lucy started crying.

Up in her room, I sang the rainbow song till she was quiet again, which took forever. Then I laid her down, stroked her back for a while and tiptoed away to downstairs.

I pressed play.

The music: I knew every note.

The credits: permanently printed on my brain.

PRODUCED BY MERVYN LEROY
DIRECTED BY VICTOR FLEMING

The action: Dorothy and Toto running down the road away from Almira Gulch.

Nanna and I knew all the words. "She isn't coming yet Toto…" We used to say them at the same time as Dorothy.

Then Lucy cried a second time. I dragged myself up to her room to see what was wrong. She needed a new nappy and her sleep-suit was dirty so I changed that too. Then I warmed a bottle of milk in the microwave, just in case she was hungry, checking the temperature on the back of my hand like Mum had shown me. And when I took it back to Lucy she was smiling and gurgling. I lifted her onto my lap to feed her.

Downstairs, the phone rang, but I let the answering machine take it.

When Lucy finished the milk she was wide awake, baby-talking and looking at her hands, like they were the most amazingest things in the world. Then I put her on my shoulder and rubbed her back until she burped. She would have let me stand there all night rocking her and singing songs, but I didn't have the energy, so I laid her in the cot again, with the musical Humpty Dumpty mobile dancing above her head and tiptoed away.

The answering machine bleeped and I pressed the play button, just in case it was Mum.

It was a man's voice. "Hey, gorgeous," he said.

I froze.

"Change of plan. The curry house is closed. I'm on my way to Les Amants. Meet me there? I'll try your mobile."

Les Amants is this fancy French restaurant across from the park, strictly for hand holding couples only. I pressed 'play' again, not quite able to believe my ears.

"Hey gorgeous, change of plan - The curry house is closed…"

And again. "Hey gorgeous, change of plan …"

But there was no mistake. The voice was my dad.

And I don't know what upset me more; that she was seeing HIM or that she was lying about it. After everything we'd been through. "How could she do this to me?"

Upstairs, Lucy started crying but all I could hear was Dad's voice in my head. I wanted to ring his mobile and tell him to get lost, except that I never wanted to speak to him again.

Lucy's crying got louder and I couldn't ignore her forever.

"There there, Lucy Locket," I said, trying to sound calm and not totally freaked out. I bent over the cot to pick her up and just as I did, without any warning, she sicked milky vomit down her clothes and onto her bed. I should have changed her again and then rocked her back to sleep, but lollipops and lullabies were the last things on my brain. And instead, I left her.

It was only supposed to be for a minute. Just long enough to phone Mum and tell her that I didn't want to be there any more, being the one in charge while SHE was off, new dress, new hair, with HIM… It was All. So. Wrong.

Mum's mobile didn't have a signal, so I phoned the Eastern Tandoori and they weren't answering. I pressed redial, redial and redial, and still nothing. Then I pulled out the telephone directory to look for the number of Les Amants, but if she was there, with HIM, what would I say?

"What do I do?" I said, grinding my teeth, breathing sharply and trying not to be upset. Our lovely few months meant nothing if she took HIM back. "Think," I told myself. "Calm down and think. One, two, three, four, five, six, seven…"

That's when I saw Nanna's blood stain on the carpet.

"No way are you ever coming back in this house." … I pulled on my pumps… "Thieving, lying, drunk. I hate you." … I grabbed my jacket … "I'm not letting you ruin my life any more," … and I left. Out the door. Down the road. Running and practically in town, only stopping because I was out of breath.

Some boozed up old dossers in a doorway called me over. They wanted to talk to me. One of them offered me a swig of his cider, but I wouldn't touch it with a bargepole. I learned my lesson about drinking, the hard way. There was a stone in my pocket, a big one; granite

I think, with a white line running around its middle, like a vein. It was cold and solid and it had been there since before Nanna's accident. I wrapped my hand round it, ready to throw if I needed to, but the dossers were too drunk to attack me.

I backed away and started running again.

When I got to the Eastern Tandoori, the windows were covered in newspaper and there was a notice stuck on the door which read 'WE ARE NOW CLOSED'. I tried the handle anyway, and knocked. I knocked on the door and the window, and I shouted "Let me in!" because I really wanted it to be open and to be wrong about Mum and HIM and Les Amants, but no matter how much I willed it not to be true, it so obviously was.

The stone started to burn in my hand. My skin was hot and tingling and my fingers twitched. I thought about throwing it, except didn't want to. That stone was my friend, and I wanted to keep it forever, with my other stones. But the burning got too much, too intense. And I don't know what came over me. I took a step back, and suddenly, there was my stone, flying in slow motion. Through the air. Through the glass. Out of sight.

The glass didn't break properly; cracks appeared around the hole, and I waited, in freeze frame with my mouth hanging open, for the glass to properly smash and for Mum to suddenly appear telling me I'd got it all wrong.

Except it didn't, and she didn't.

The alarm went off and I wanted my stone back. I reached through the hole, and that's when the glass did come crashing down. I put my arms up over my head to protect myself, but I don't remember anything else about that night.

I woke up on another day, in hospital with bandages on my arms, cuts on my head and my long black curls hacked off.

Mum was there.

The first thing I said was, "Where's Lucy?"

"Oh thank god you're all right," Mum said, trying to hold my hand.

"Where's Lucy?" I said again. "Is she all right?"

"She's with Mrs Scott," said Mum. "And yes, she's fine." Mrs Scott was our busy-body neighbour. She phoned the police when she saw the door open, and by the time Mum got home, a policewoman and a social worker were waiting in the kitchen with a very wide-awake Lucy.

"Ruby, what were you thinking?"

I looked away from Mum, out of the window. There was nothing to see, just a brick wall and more windows.

"Why did you leave Lucy? Why didn't you phone? Be honest. I need to know what you were thinking."

Honesty works two ways, I thought.

"Were you drinking again?" she said, after a while.

"No I bloody wasn't!" I snapped. How could she even think such a thing? So we argued then, about drinking and lying and who was to blame for everything and somewhere in the middle of it all I blurted out, "And how IS Dad?"

Mum stopped, pre-sentence, mouth open and eyes wide. Guilty. "How do you know?"

"Check your answering machine."

And Mum said, "Oh baby, I'm sorry. I'm so sorry. So so sorry. But it's not what you think…"

I pulled the covers over my head and waited till she left.

I refused to see her after that.

Siobhan, my nurse, sat with me at visiting because I didn't have anyone else. She told me stories about all her little brothers and sisters and the funny things they did. It made me miss Lucy so badly it hurt. And then one day she brought me a little mauve note book and a chunky blue pen. She said she always wrote letters to her little brothers and sisters and it helped her not to miss them. She said it would help me too.

"What am I supposed to write?" I said.

"Anything you like," she said. "It's always better out than in."

She sounded like my nanna. So I started writing to Lucy telling her about the hospital and stuff. The letters weren't for sending and I didn't let anyone look at my book, not even Siobhan.

When my arms were better, Mum and Helen came to collect me and I went home to pack. Apart from clothes and a toothbrush, I took my stones, my Wizard of Oz DVD and Lucy's Book. I didn't talk to Mum and when she tried to push a letter into my hands I let it drop to the floor. I didn't see Lucy because she was with Mrs Scott. There was no sign of Dad.

Outside, a white puffy cloud drifted across the blue sky. I watched the birds. There were tits, sparrows and magpies. I could hear a thrush too, but I couldn't see it. The tits were the prettiest, and popped in and out of a nesting box on a tree. "If you could fly, you would never fall," I said.

Mrs Stein said, "I'm sorry?"

She wasn't meant to hear me. "I was just thinking out loud," I said.

And her face softened. "Grief is a very difficult emotion," she said, obviously thinking that birds flying and Nanna's death were somehow linked. "You must miss your grandmother very much."

"I don't want to talk about Nanna," I said, folding my arms. When would they all realise, talking wouldn't change anything?

"Okay," she said. "Let's move on. Let's talk about Pearl."

"Oh yes, Pearl!" I said, emphasising the P.

She raised an eyebrow. "I have already spoken to Pearl this morning."

"And what did she say?" I bet she didn't tell about the chalkstone, or about calling me names.

"Actually, she said you two had gotten off on the wrong foot and she doesn't want to take this any further."

"Oh!" I said, surprised.

"So I'd like you to find a time to apologise to each other," said Mrs Stein. "It will be good for you both."

I bit the inside of my cheek, waiting for Mrs Stein to tell me when we were supposed to endure our moment of humiliating sorryness. But she never did.

"So we'll leave it at that for now, Ruby," she said.

"Oh," I said, again. "Thank you." I stood up and walked towards the door trying to stop a smile growing on my face. I never, not in a million years, expected to walk away without some kind of punishment.

And then Mrs Stein coughed pointedly. I turned round. She was holding a letter out at arms length. Mum's letter. The one I didn't want. Mrs Stein didn't say anything, just held it there for me to take.

So I took it. And without even bothering to look inside, I ripped it in two and dropped the pieces on the floor. I turned to leave.

"At the end of the week, I'd like you to start play therapy," said Mrs Stein. That was, like, her parting shot; perfectly timed as I closed the door.

PLAY THERAPY? I am thirteen years old and I do not need play therapy.

Dear Lucy,

Nanna used to say, "Get in the garden and smell the roses." It was the place she loved most in the whole world. She didn't just mean her garden either. She took me to Kew, which is a beautiful big garden in London where you can walk in the trees. She took me to Virginia Water, a huge park with a lake and woods and a garden with cabbage plants looking like flowers. And she took me to Mrs Bagley's garden to show me the sweet peas climbing all over the fence.

Nanna said she had a little drum inside of her which banged every time she felt good. And whenever you were in a garden, it didn't matter which one, you could almost hear that drum beating ta-dum ta-dum ta-dum...

And when you turned to look at her face, her smile was so infectious, you couldn't help but feel happy too.

But her own garden was the nicest garden of them all, because Nanna had grown everything, "with love and a pair of hands," she said. Flowers, fruit, vegetables and wildlife; everything wanted to live in Nanna's garden. She had frogs in the undergrowth, blackbirds nesting in her honeysuckle and a Robin who came back year after year.

She trained the Robin to ask for food, by leaving seeds and blueberries on her kitchen windowsill every day for weeks. One day she didn't put any out and when the robin came along and saw no food, he tapped his beak on the window.

I was there and I saw it! It's true.

She was going to train it to sit on her hand...

I wanted to write more, but my eyes dripped on the paper and smudged the ink.

Chapter 8

Fridays were half days, and in the afternoon everyone got a choice about what they did. On my first Friday, Amy and Rachel had visitors and the others were going ice skating. What I really wanted to do was to borrow the DVD player and watch MY film, in MY room, on MY own, but Mrs Stein wanted me to see Danielle, the play therapist.

At dinner, I picked at the food.

"Are you all right?" asked Lily.

"I'm not hungry," I said.

"Well that's a surprise," she said. "You usually tuck it away! I was beginning to wonder if you had hollow legs. Do you ever put on weight?"

"It's genetic," I said, bored, because it was one of my mum's favourite themes too. Mum only had to look at a calorie for her to get fat, whereas my dad could eat anything and only ever look like a total bean-pole.

Lily laughed. "You don't know how lucky you are." She patted her enormous belly, and then said, "Pearl's like you. Eat anything she can."

I looked across at Pearl's plate piled high with mashed potato, and Pearl shovelling it in like there was no tomorrow. She glared at me. Clearly, having stick thin-ness in common was not a bond either of us welcomed.

"I'm not well," I said, "Can I go and lie down in my room?"

Lily shook her head and smiled. "Not today, Missy."

"But Lily, I feel sick."

"It's just nerves."

"I'm not nervous though," I said.

"And you're not missing play therapy either." Lily stood up and collected the empty plates.

"I've got a really bad belly ache," I said, pulling a sickly face, holding my tummy and acting my head off. But Lily didn't believe me this time and disappeared into the kitchen.

I was left with Miss Wicked Witch of the West and her fan club. They ignored me, but spoke in really loud voices about their ice skating trip, obviously wanting me to hear. Pearl told Bianca and Scarlet how she could do a waltz jump and what a loop was and why it was so easy when you were a natural. Bianca and Scarlet told Pearl how clever she was and begged her to teach them too.

Like it was real?

Then Pearl stopped, MID LOOP, and smiled a fake smile at me. "You'll be all right," she said, wrinkling her nose.

"What?" I said, waiting for the punch line.

"You can take your little fwend to meet Danny. Hold hands." She said it in a patronising babyish voice.

"What are you talking about?" I said.

"Your invisible fwend," she said. "That one you're ALWAYS talking to. Skitzo." She snapped the last word, and it hung in the air for a second or two before Bianca and Scarlet practically fell off their chairs laughing.

I cringed, pushed my uneaten dinner away and left.

Outside in the garden, I punched the wall with the side of my fist.

"Witch," I said, because that's what she reminded me of, with her green make-up and black lips. All she needed was a pointy hat. And all I needed was to be somewhere else.

Nanna would have said, "There's something good in everything and everyone." I just couldn't think what it could possibly be in Pearl.

I lifted my eyes and saw roses; red and yellow and pink, all neatly clipped and loosely tied to garden canes with string to stop them from flopping. And below the roses, a row of large stones framing the border. I walked over, bent down and picked up a very round sandstone, more like a giant pebble.

"You'll do," I said.

Nanna and I had some of our best chats in her garden. Chinwags she called them. I'd help her weed and she'd talk about the best plants for insects, because the more insects you have the more birds you attract. And then we'd sit back in the deck chairs drinking lemonade through straws, watching sparrows swoop down for their insect lunch. In between counting the birds, Nanna liked to make a point of telling me there was nothing like homemade lemonade. "Healthy, refreshing and delicious," she'd say. "And it doesn't get you drunk." The only times Nanna ever said anything negative was when she talked about my dad.

Even when she fell over in the garden, stumbling and scraping her arm and bruising her body all the way down her right side, she didn't complain. I helped her back to the chairs and gave her some sweet lemonade and her white face got its colour back.

"Are you okay, Nanna?" I was worried.

"Peachy," she said.

"But look at your arm," I said. "Maybe we should phone an ambulance."

"I'm fine, Ducky. Thank you for helping me. I appreciate that."

And then after a few minutes, she said, "Look at those bumble bees dancing on the lavender. Isn't that a beautiful thing?"

I hugged her and said, "I'll always be here for you, Nanna." And I meant it too.

Blinking away the tears, I looked down at the stone in my hand. Close up, you could see lines. I knew enough to know that these were the layers of sand, all pressed together. And I knew it was round because of all the rolling and bouncing it did on the sea bed. I didn't know how it had ended up in a garden at High Fell.

I put the stone in my bag. When I looked back towards the house, Lily was waving to me through a window, pointing at her watch.

Chapter 9

I don't know what I was expecting, but the play therapy room wasn't it. If the rest of school was boring brown Kansas, the play therapy room was Oz.

When I opened the door, the colours hit me. Sunset orange daisies in a bright red vase, stood against summer yellow walls, with emerald green spider plants dripping babies over the sky-blue cupboards. The floor was shiny and wooden, except for the bits where people walked and the shine had worn off; which felt lived in, and nice. And it smelled sweet, of airwick or something.

Danielle held a folder with my name in black capital letters across the top. "Ruby, would you like to take that pack off and sit down?" She was small, wearing scruffbag jeans and silver old lady glasses, even though she wasn't old.

I sat down, but kept my backpack.

Danielle told me about play therapy and how it was up to me to decide what we did and what we talked about. She had these rules on a laminate which I was supposed to read, but I didn't. I skimmed the words, and got the general idea; I talked, she listened. And no one was judging me. Blah blah blah…

"So what's in these cupboards?" I said, standing up. Because if I was going to spend the afternoon there I needed to find something to do, other than NOT talking. I opened doors. There were toys, puppets, masks, clay and board games. Some with unlikely names: 'Know Your Limit', 'Family Mediation' and 'Impulse Control.' I pulled out some lame brick stacking game. "What about this one?" I said, because I already knew how to play and it didn't need me to talk.

"Good choice," said Danielle.

I sat down and tipped the bricks onto the table. Danielle built the tower, while I watched.

"Do you want to go first?" she said, when the tower was finished.

I took a brick from near the bottom of the stack.

Danielle smiled. "Living dangerously," she said, and then took a SAFE one from near the top.

I took another.

Then Danielle.

And so on.

All without further comment. Perfect.

I played the same game with Nanna when I was a little kid. I played a lot of games with Nanna when Dad was away and Mum worked weekends. I probably spent more time with Nanna than anyone.

Apart from playing games, gardening, bird spotting and watching the Wizard of Oz, Nanna took me to museums, parks and the seaside. She showed me how to bake cakes, taught me how to read and said that life was all about being happy and doing things you love. The thing I loved doing most of all in the whole world was making up plays for Nanna and me to perform.

They were always called things like, The Old Lady and the Witch, The Princess and the Dragon, or The Wicked Queen and the Magic Cat, and I always had the most lines to say. Mum and Dad would sit on the edge of their seats, sometimes crying with laughter, and when it was over they would clap and shout "encore!"

Nanna said that when I grew up I should be an actor. Dad was very enthusiastic about that; said that I could win an Oscar, and when I was rich and famous I would be able to buy him a case of Chateau Lafitte (which is a very expensive wine and costs about a hundred thousand pounds just for one bottle). Nanna counted to ten and told me there was more to life than silly bottles of wine.

I touched a brick - didn't even move it - but the whole thing CRASHED into a clattering heap. It made me jump, literally, and bricks spilled all over the floor. I froze, just for a second. The noise, followed by the silence made me feel sick inside. My mouth was dry and my hands were shaking. I got down on my knees so Danielle couldn't see my face, and I collected all the bricks and put them back on the table.

"It's all right," said Danielle. "They're just bricks."

I started stacking them up again, building a wall. Danielle watched me from the other side, but I tried not to think about anything and just concentrated on getting the wall really straight and perfect, nothing out of place and no gaps. And when I was finished, I took my backpack off and put it on the chair next to me.

Chapter 10

Back in my room, there was a pile of clean clothes on my bed. Next to them was a roll of sellotape and the pieces of mum's torn letter. I could only guess Lily had left it all there in the mistaken belief that after a session of play therapy I would want to read the stupid thing.

I didn't.

I took off my backpack and put my clothes away and wondered how long it would be before tea time, because I was extremely hungry and regretted leaving my lunch.

I looked out of the window. Outside in the garden, Amy was showing her visitor around. He was a man with a scar across his cheek and greasy grey hair. I watched them for a while. They looked awkward together and hardly said anything while they walked. Obviously neither of them appreciated the beautiful garden. They didn't even look at the flowers or the view, and their walk was more like a march than something they could enjoy.

When they reached the bench, they sat down and he took a brown envelope from his pocket. He gave it to Amy. She opened it up to find an iPod Nano inside. The LOOK on her face! She went from miserable and bored as sin to totally ecstatic in less than a millisecond. She even hugged old scar-face. He was embarrassed and twitchy, but she didn't notice because she was too busy fiddling with her new toy. When he spoke, you could see that he had teeth missing. I wondered if he was her dad.

Amy looked up and saw me, so I moved away.

I wasn't jealous or anything. I didn't want a Nano, and her dad looked like some seedy no hoper who hung around outside the job centre fishing fag ends out of the gutter.

Mum's letter was still there on my bed. I picked it up, and put it down. I wanted to read it, but I didn't want lies. I picked up one half of the envelope again and peered inside. There was a photo in there, as well as the letter. I pulled the two pieces of photo from each half of the envelope and put them together. It was like Pearl's pink box all over again, except that this time the severed photo was mine. It was Lucy. And I started to cry. Not real sobs or anything, just water falling from my eyes.

"What a stupid cow you are, Ruby Garnett," I said, touching my sister's little sausage arms. She was smiling too. I should never have left her that night.

I pulled the pieces of letter from their torn envelope and opened them flat, putting them next to each other on the bed. I could read it without the sellotape.

Dear Ruby,

I wanted to come with you and see you settled into your new school, but I knew you wouldn't let me so I am writing instead. Because whatever else has happened between us, you need to know that I do care.

I am sorry I lied. I didn't mean to; it's just that I didn't want to upset you. Dad and I were tying up loose ends, NOT getting back together. I should have been honest with you. But I've not been a very good communicator, have I? Too wound up in my own problems to notice that you just weren't coping. I had no idea that things at school were so bad until I met Mr Hickory.

I now know about the letters home you kept from me and the detentions you never turned up for, and I'm only telling you this to clear the air. What's done is done. I am not cross. I'm just sorry for not realising how unhappy you were, and I promise it will never happen again.

You were such a support when Lucy was born and I don't know how I would have managed that alone. I am going to miss you so much. I know you probably don't believe that at the moment, but it's 100% true. Ruby, you are very important to me and I would never do anything to deliberately hurt you.

Will you write and tell me what it's like at your new school? About your new friends and the teachers? Please tell me everything. And as soon as you are ready, I would like to come and visit you. Please say I can.

They tell me that High Fell is in a lovely place. I'm not going back to work after my maternity leave, so I can come any time.

I LOVE YOU VERY MUCH.

Mum x

PS The picture of Lucy was taken at baby singing. She is just like you were.

Some things leave you hollow and empty and Mum's letter was one of them. When I was little I remember her saying "I love you" every single night before I went to sleep. But when she got her promotion at work, it got forgotten somewhere in amongst the last minute preparations for directors' lunches and work parties. I wondered if she stopped feeling it too. But here she was, writing the very words I wanted to hear.

I read them over and over again.

"But she met up with Dad," I said. "New hair, new clothes, new smile. After everything he did. How could she?"

Dear Lucy,

This is a true story about Nanna, just so you know what she was like.

One year she grew raspberries and redcurrants. I remember them being big and juicy and I wanted to eat them all from the bush.

But Nanna said, "They need another day."

When I wasn't happy about that, Nanna said, "Let's go brambling instead."

She always knew the right thing to do, so we got on a train to the South Downs and took our plastic pots with lids, and found a place where the blackberries were fat and sweet, and the sun shone. We stuffed our faces good and proper, then sat on the grass happy, and looked at the view.

When we got home, Nanna said we needed to pick the ripest raspberries and redcurrants because she had a plan.

I was fruited out and it must have shown on my face, but Nanna said I was the bestest fruit picker she had ever known, so I took a big bowl and filled it to overflowing. Then I watched Nanna make all those blackberries and raspberries and redcurrants into a delicious summer pudding.

Next morning, she turned the pudding onto a plate and she was about to cut into it when she suddenly stopped.

"Ducky! Cream!" she cried. "We need some cream." I really didn't mind about the cream, but she

insisted, so we went to the Spar and they were out of cream and so we caught a bus into town. Nanna talked non-stop to total strangers nearly all the way there, telling them how we'd been to the Downs and what a great brambler I was and how we'd come back to find our own fruit ready and how the recipe for Summer pudding was so easy "with a bit of stale bread and a tiny dollop of know how…"

Nanna was probably the happiest person alive.

In Marks and Spencer's she chose a tub of Cornish clotted cream. "Mum won't thank us for this," she said, puffing her cheeks out like a fat bloater, but bought it anyway and said we'd earned it.

Then, on the way home, something happened.

I don't quite know how. She fell again. She went off the kerb and landed in the road. Cars screeched to a halt and all these people came running over to see if she was all right. She kept saying, "Don't worry, I'm fine," and tried to get rid of them. But there was blood on her head and someone called an ambulance and they made her go to hospital.

I went with her and phoned Mum at work. She came along later and a nurse asked Mum lots of questions about Nanna.

Nobody thought about asking me.

And when they spoke to Nanna, it was in a slow, loud voice like they thought she was deaf, or stupid. "Do. You. Ever. Feel dizzy. Or light headed? What did you eat. For breakfast? Have you. Ever. Fallen before?" Things like that.

Nanna insisted she was all right, and told them to stop making a fuss and send her home.

They made her stay the night, and next day before they let her go they gave her cards with appointments to see some other special doctors called a cardiologist *and a neurologist, and when Nanna got home she said, "What I need is a clumsyologist." Then she tore up her appointments and said, "Now where's that summer pudding?"*

That's what Nanna was like.

Love you,

Ruby x

Chapter 11

Sometimes, writing to Lucy didn't help. My legs twitched with tiredness, my skin itched to be scratched, the duvet kept falling off and I couldn't get comfortable.

By morning, I looked like Almira Gulch (before she was the Wicked Witch of the West), with massive black bags under my eyes. And I was late for breakfast. I sat down with Amy and Rachel and listened to them bragging about which visitor delivered the most. Amy had her iPod Nano of course, and apparently it was already half full of music. Rachel's visitor, a social worker, had taken her shopping for new clothes, even though she absolutely didn't need any more. (No one needs that many clothes.) On the other table, Scarlet and Bianca were sat either side of Pearl, who had extremely puffy eyes and a very red nose.

Scarlet said, "Don't worry. It'll work out."

And then Bianca said, "Yeah, you'll be all right."

Then Scarlet said, "And you've always got us."

And then Bianca, "But someone will want you. Eventually…"

And Pearl howled, obviously not for the first time.

Lily came in with fresh toast in one hand and a box of tissues in the other. She gave me the toast and went over to Pearl, moving Bianca so she could sit in her seat. Pearl leaned into Lily's humungous chest.

"Come on, Luvvy. It wasn't the right one for you, that's all."

"No one wants me," sniffed Pearl. "What's wrong with me?"

"Nothing's wrong with you. Foster placements are hard to find, especially for older children. You know that. But there's nothing wrong with you. You're a lovely girl."

Pearl's upset made me wonder why she needed a foster home when she had such a massive family? How come she couldn't go and live with one of the fun-loving gang on her bedroom wall? Out of all those people in stupid umbrella hats, waving at the camera from log flumes and posing next to castle ruins, someone must want her.

I thought back to my letter from Mum. Whatever I felt about her, she wanted me back home, and I didn't doubt for a minute I would go.

Tom came in and clapped his hands to get our attention. He had a camera bag strapped across his chest and he was wearing a baseball cap back to front. "Right now, Ladies. We've got two options today. One, you can stay here and be boooored, or two, you can come bowling with me and Ali. Hooray! Anyone who gets a strike wins a treat, and anyone who beats me will have to write a hundred lines, I MUST NOT BEAT TOM AT BOWLING."

Even Pearl's face managed to crack a smile.

Tom looked at his watch. "The minibus will be leaving in ten minutes, so if there's anything you need to do, do it now."

I didn't join in the rush to get out of the room because I didn't want to go bowling. Tom sat down next to me. "Are you not going to get ready?"

I shrugged. "I'm not coming."

"Sure you are. You need to join in, Ruby. Make friends. We'll have a lovely time; get some ice creams and take silly pictures. I'll even let you have copies, just so you never forget what a brilliant day you've had."

When he said that, I realised where Pearl's Polaroids had come from. All those faces on her wall weren't family at all. They were people who were paid to take her out.

"I really DON'T want to go," I said.

"But everyone is going," he said, as if that was a good enough reason, when actually it was the perfect reason not to go.

I didn't say anything; just gave him my best 'whatever' look and sank my teeth into the cold toast.

Tom did a fake sulk, but he didn't argue and said, "Well I suppose you do look kind of tired."

And Lily, who was clearing away around me agreed. "Did you sleep at all?"

"Not much," I said. Lily and Tom were both staring at me, checking out the size of my eye bags. "I read my mum's letter," I said, by way of explanation.

Lily nodded. "Then maybe a day on your own is not such a bad idea. Go back to bed and I'll wake you up for lunch. We can play a game later, if you like."

I think I might have managed a half genuine smile.

The others thundered back down stairs. Pearl was wearing her black stack boots and a black lacy glove. Her face was heavily made up with the usual black lipstick and dark green eye shadow, and her puffy red eyes were lost behind the thick black mascara and false lashes. She'd also put extensions in her hair so it was wilder and way bigger than normal. The others made some effort, but Pearl stood out in the crowd.

They were all loud and excitable, honking like a herd of wild geese at full volume about their bowling names and how they were going to thrash Tom and how very hilarious they were. Not.

And then they were gone.

I went up to my room, and climbed back into bed.

Later, Lily brought me a cheese sandwich and some crisps. She asked, "Do you want to make friends here?"

"No," I replied, which couldn't possibly have been a surprise. "Anyone can see they all hate me." Even though it sounded like I was feeling sorry for myself, I wasn't.

Lily said, "You can't just lock yourself away like this all the time. People want to get to know you. And you need friends. Everyone needs friends."

"You're wrong," I said. Friends are unpredictable and anyway, they get you into trouble.

"Let them get to know you." She picked up my Wizard of Oz DVD. "This film for example; why don't you bring it down one evening and we can all watch it together."

"No!" I shouted, grabbing it from her hands. "It's mine! Leave it alone." My film was just too special to share, especially with people I didn't like.

Lily stared at me, but I looked away, regretting my explosion. And then there was like, this FOREVER silence, and that was somehow worse than the noise.

Chapter 12

The next time I went to play therapy, I took Mum's letter.

"Do you want to see a picture of my sister?" I pulled Lucy's sellotaped photo from my bag and passed it to Danielle.

She lifted her glasses to get a better look. "What's her name?"

"Lucy," I said. "I chose it; after my nanna, Lucinda."

"That's a pretty name. And she looks like you."

I had Mum's letter in my bag and fished down to get it, tossing it onto the table between us. "You can read that if you want."

Danielle picked it up and held the pieces together while she read.

I looked out of the window. There were three magpies; one for sorrow, two for joy, three for a girl... And then I looked back at Danielle.

When she eventually finished, she said, "How did you feel when you read it?"

I tried to remember. "Twistified," I said after a while.

"Twistified?"

"Sort of, you want it to be one thing but you feel like it's another, and it tangles you up in a knot," I said.

"Like things are confusing and difficult to understand?"

"Yeah, because Mum changes. Sometimes she's like this and then she isn't. She's someone else. I don't know who she is."

"How would you describe your mum?" Danielle said.

I thought about her rushing to work in the morning, coming home late, writing fridge notes so she didn't forget what she had to do. I thought about the last few birthdays and Christmases when Mum asked for a list of the presents I wanted, when all I really wanted was for her to surprise me, to spend time with me. I remembered the times I tried to tell her about the thieving, and how because she would hardly stay still long enough to listen, she never knew. "Always in a rush," I said.

"You feel your mum didn't make time for you?" said Danielle.

"Well she did… but then she didn't… and when she left work it all changed again. We got on better and …"

I remembered how we shopped for baby clothes and how I went to ante-natal classes with her. I remembered how we painted Lucy's bedroom in just one day and shared a pizza delivery for tea because we were too tired to cook.

"And?" coaxed Danielle.

I shook my head. "But she lied to me. How can I trust her? She got all tarted up to meet my dad. After everything that happened with him. He walked out on us you know. Not once. Twice. The first time, he left without even saying goodbye; no phone number, no address, so we didn't even know if we'd see him again. It was like he died, or something. It was awful. I cried and cried and Mum said she would never forgive him. And then she took him back. Why would she do that? How do I know she's not planning to get back with him

55

again? And even though she says she's giving up work, how do I know she means it? She's a workaholic. Is that a word? Because if it's not, it should be."

And then Danielle said, "You feel let down."

I shrugged. "Yeah, something like that; because you just want people to be honest, to be straight, you know? Otherwise it's just messing with your head. And I don't need that any more."

I don't even remember how old I was when Dad asked me to get him some money from Nanna's purse. I took notes and coins, and her post office card. And handed them over, pleased with my helpful little self. "Nanna won't want you to mention this in front of Mum," he'd say, winking. "So best not mention it at all." I loved us being partners in this big amazing secret, like we were only doing it as some immense surprise for Mum. By the time I was old enough to know it was stealing, I was too involved to say no. When he left home the first time, it all stopped, but I have never been able to tell anyone and it's been messing with my head ever since.

"Yeah, people can let you down really bad," I said.

Danielle nodded. She was about to say something, but I interrupted.

"Except Nanna. She never ever let me down."

Danielle looked at me for a while and then calmly said, "Do you think change is a bad thing? I mean, often people change for the better."

I folded my arms and looked out of the window. And then nobody said anything at all.

Eventually, I got bored. I stood up, went over to the cupboard where the brick game was, and opened the door. The game wasn't there. In fact, none of the games were there, so I checked out the other cupboards and realised everything had moved.

"Where have the games gone?" I said, in a slightly higher pitched and more desperate voice than I would have liked.

"Over there, behind the sofa, the cupboard on the far left," said Danielle, as if it was totally okay for things to be different.

On the floor in front of the cupboard was a large purple tray full of dry sand. "Sand?" I said, in that freaked out voice again.

"Some people like to play with sand," said Danielle.

"Aren't we a bit old for buckets and spades?" There wasn't actually a bucket or spade anywhere in sight.

"We often have much younger children than you at High Fell…"

"Yeah, the Munchkins," I laughed. Amy and Rachel. That's what they reminded me of.

"…But being the oldest here doesn't stop you from using the sand tray, if you want to."

There were some plastic animals and Lego people half buried. I certainly didn't want to play with toys. But the sun streamed through the window and some of the tiny sand grains sparkled like miniature diamonds. I put my hands flat and wiggled my fingers and I got a memory of Brighton Beach in my brain.

I thought, I must tell Lucy about that day.

Then I scrunched up my fingers and lifted my hands into the air. The dry sand grains sprinkled down like magic dust, making little tiny dunes in the tray below. I did it again and again, totally rapt by the changing shape of the little piles. Every now and again, a Lego person or plastic animal would find its way into my hand, and when it did, I put it to one side until all the people and all the animals were lined up in a row watching me.

The baby dunes got bigger and bigger, until eventually they couldn't get any bigger and the sand just kept falling down the sides of the slope. I opened my bag, took out my stones one by one and lay them in a circle around the dunes, and then continued to pour the sand inside the wall.

The Lego girl with black hair, yellow face and a red body sat and watched me. She was the only girl there, all alone. And for some reason, looking at her made me feel sad, so I picked her up and plunged her deep into the middle of the dune where nobody could see her, and I didn't have to feel sad any more.

Danielle was watching me. I felt babyish then, playing in sand, so I stood up and collected my stones and put them away in my backpack.

"That's a very impressive collection," said Danielle.

"It's taken me years," I said. I glanced at the clock. There was still time to kill before I could go, so I took out one stone and gave it to Danielle to hold. It was the stone I'd found in the garden at High Fell. "Can you see the layers? It's sandstone, which means it started just like that." I pointed at the dry sand in the tray. "Don't you think that's amazing?"

"It's amazing how things change over time," said Danielle.

The bell went off. I picked up Mum's letter from the table. "Should I write back to her?" I asked.

"Do you want to?"

I stopped and considered the idea, for about five whole seconds. "Not really."

Dear Lucy,

Nanna took me to the seaside. I'm going to take you there one day.

We played in the sand and jumped over the waves. I had a donkey ride and fish and chips out of the paper and pink candy floss on a stick.

Nanna said "Life doesn't get any better than this."

And when you were with Nanna, the mud squelching between your toes, or the salty taste of the sea or the feeling of being dry and warm after a dip in the cold sea... well, they were all reasons to be happy.

On the way home, I said, "I've got sand in my shoes."

"I've got sand in my wrinkles," Nanna said.

"But I've got enough to build a sandcastle," I said

"And I've got enough to make a beach," Nanna said.

"Well I've got enough for a desert," I said

"Then I shall buy a camel..." laughed Nanna. "With two humps."

The idea of Nanna riding a camel made me laugh so much, my face hurt. The other passengers in our carriage must have thought we were crazy people.

Love you,

Ruby x

I remembered that day.

When I got home and Nanna went back to her house, it stopped being funny. It stopped because Nanna was like sunshine; when the sun went down, everything went dark.

There was Mum, stressing. "Ruby, you've got sand everywhere and dirt all over the bathroom."

And there was Dad, guzzling whisky and not even bothering to get out of his chair, moaning, "You're not going out with her again if this is what happens…"

You'd have thought they'd be grateful, but they weren't.

Chapter 13

The next day was warm and the sky was totally blue. At lunch, Mrs Stein announced we were ALL going for a walk to Fellside Meadow wherever that was. The ALL bit was so obviously directed at me, and despite the company and the ever increasing black bags under my eyes, I wanted to be outside in the fresh air and away from school.

"We'll take pads and pencils, and some games and make an afternoon of it," said Mrs Stein. "Back in time for tea."

Everyone had to take a bag with their own sketch book and snacks. Tom had his camera bag and another one with balls and frisbees. Mrs Stein and Alison had drinks and first aid, and Alison was wearing wellies. For once, my backpack didn't look out of place.

"Oh look!" declared Pearl. "The freak's coming with us."

Bianca was just about to find her funny, but this time I answered back. "Yeah, I wanted to see if it was true."

"See if what's true?" said Pearl.

"That you run like a chicken. Cos that's what Bianca reckons." (It was just the first thing that came into my brain.)

Pearl turned to Bianca. "You said I run like a chicken?"

"I never did," said Bianca, outraged.

"So why did she say it?" said Pearl.

"Because she's mental."

"Yeah but why that? It's too random…"

Bianca tried to reason with Pearl, but Pearl didn't believe her, and we walked down the road with them bickering away.

When we went around the bend, a totally awesome view sort of smacked me in the face and I forgot about Pearl. Immediately below us was an open flat area of green fields with a twisty river running down the middle and into the sea. Behind the fields on the other side was a row of rocky hills with tiny houses and white dots for sheep.

"That's Morecambe Bay over there," said Tom. "And down there where it's flat, that's the Lyth Valley. Isn't it beautiful?"

The lane veered right, down into the valley, but we climbed over a wooden stile on the left into a sloping field with lots of yellow buttercups and pink flowering clover. There were trees around the edge and a trickling stream along the side.

Bianca sat down in the flowers and grass. I thought she was sulking at first, but she started drawing and after a while I realised she was totally engrossed and not bothered about anything except her art.

Everyone else went for the stream, including me. It was shallow and only a few feet wide. The others took off their shoes and socks and splashed each other and Mrs Stein let them. In a proper school, teachers would be having massive freak-outs over broken glass and tetanus or foot and mouth disease. All we got was a warning about not wandering downstream because of some waterfall.

I went upstream a little way to be on my own and found a large boulder to sit on. I took off my backpack and started trying to draw the scenery, wishing I was good at art. Except that my wish didn't suddenly come true and I was just as rubbish as always. So instead, I got into the water and collected stones, singing to myself. "Where pebbles are like lemon drops and streams fizz just like soda pops, that's where you'll find me..." In a short time, I had red, orange, yellowy brown, blueish and grey stones arranged in an arc on the green grassy bank. I just needed something purple to complete my rainbow, and moved upstream a little further, searching.

That was when I saw the kingfisher. A flash of electric blue flew past me and landed on a branch. I had never in all my life seen a kingfisher before but I knew about them, obviously. Nanna told me they were the most elegant birds she had ever seen and the Greeks thought they were a symbol of peace and inner calm. I could never have imagined a bird so beautiful.

My eyes took in every detail; the vivid blue back feathers and orangey chest, the white throat, red legs and dagger-like bill. It looked at me, and then whistled, 'chi-keeeee,' before flying downstream. I watched it go, wondering where it went and what it would find when it got there.

I felt happy and sad at the same time. If only Nanna could have seen it.

But then Tom shouted, "Okay ladies, the party's over. Let the games begin."

I started singing again. "If happy little bluebirds fly, away from High Fell, why oh why can't I?" trying to ignore him.

Then he shouted again, really loud. "EVERYONE IS PLAYING!"

I looked up. "Do I have to?" I shouted.

"Yes you do have to. But it's not a problem because it's fun!" said Tom.

Chapter 14

I pulled my shoes onto wet feet and crammed all the stones into my backpack. Tom produced a frisbee, explained the rules of the game and just started throwing it around. Pearl didn't seem to mind looking like a fool, running and leaping to catch the silly plastic disc and when she got near me I clucked like a chicken, just to wind her up. She glared and swore at me with her finger.

Game on.

I took off my backpack and left it with Mrs Stein.

Bianca was first out. She didn't even try. I grabbed the frisbee then, and threw it to Amy who caught it and threw it to Tom.

Meanwhile, Pearl was shouting at Bianca for being out. "You're about as much use as a chocolate teapot," she complained.

It was the first time I'd heard anyone say that in a long time. It was one of my dad's little FUNNIES, and hearing Pearl use it made my spine tingle all the way down to the bottom. I lost concentration and had to dive to catch Tom's throw.

"Well caught!" shouted Tom, and Pearl shot me a filthy look.

I will not lose to her, I thought.

Next out was Amy, then Rachel, then Scarlet, which left only Tom, me and Pearl. Pearl clearly didn't want to lose against me either, but we were pretty evenly matched and it could have gone either way until Pearl started with backhands which went off in strange directions. And I found myself practically jumping through hoops to stay in the game.

In the end I missed. "That was a rubbish throw!" I shouted. "I'm not out!"

"She is!" screamed Pearl.

Tom looked at Mrs Stein for help.

"Let's call it a tie," she said.

"Sit on the fence why don't you," shouted Pearl. "That was easily mine..." and she was off, ranting on about fairness and favouritism while Mrs Stein tried to reason with her.

It was funny. This was the real Pearl. False nails and fat-lash mascara weren't nearly as important as winning. And I almost liked her for that.

Because we were all puffed out with red cheeks and sweaty faces, we had a break then. Orange juice, crisps and rich tea biscuits. Tom used the opportunity to tell unhilarious jokes which nobody laughed at and Mrs Stein looked at our sketch pads. Bianca's drawings were awesomely amazing; flowers mostly, in lots of detail. No one else had drawn anything even half as good, and Tom said that she should win an award.

Pearl scowled. "Yeah, the chocolate teapot award for frisbee uselessness."

And there it was again; the chocolate teapot, reminding me of Dad, just when I was starting to have fun. But that's how it always was with him. Every single good thing he did always had a drink attached to it, and one drink became two, became three, became four... until life was just one long drinking session. He was rude to people, he threw up in the street and sometimes I wondered if he even knew who I was. I remember one day, him looking at me through the bottom of a glass and saying, "Which one are you?"

"Are you all right, Ruby?" said Tom.

The sun was high in the sky and there was hardly a breeze, yet my arms were covered in goose pimples.

Chapter 15

When we got back to school I went to my room to sort out my new stones.

The first stone I ever owned was a raw chunk of amethyst. It looked just like a magical purple crystal plucked straight from the Earth's crust, and was the most completely beautiful thing I had ever seen. It was a present from my dad because he said it was pretty, and I was pretty. He said he wanted to buy me a ruby, but couldn't afford it and the amethyst was the next best thing. Nanna looked up amethysts in an encyclopaedia and laughed out loud when she discovered the ancient Greeks used amethysts as a cure for drunkenness.

"How appropriate," she said. "Let's hope it works."

Dad scowled at her for spoiling his gift, and I was torn between wanting to please both of them.

I told them I would use it as a good luck stone to make my dreams come true.

Dad said, "And when you're rich and famous and a big shot movie star, don't forget my bottles of Chateau Lafitte."

After he left the room, Nanna tutted. "I want you to remember this, Ruby: Being successful isn't the amount of money in the bank, or your name in the paper or expensive bottles of wine. Success is the amount of joy you feel. Nothing more, nothing less."

Every day for a year I cradled that rock in my hands and dreamed about being an actor on a stage in front of hundreds of people. I got to know every line and angle, every lump and bump and every delicate shade, from the wispiest smokiest lavender to the deepest darkest purple. Even now, even after not seeing it for seven years, if you put a hundred raw amethysts in front of me, I'd be able to tell you which one was mine.

When Dad left us the first time, the amethyst disappeared.

Chapter 16

I dreamed about seeing the amethyst again.

I was at the top of the stairs and my amethyst was at the bottom. Nanna was next to me with a bottle in her hand. The bottle had RUBY PORT written on it, and Nanna was shouting at me to get the amethyst. I was upset and crying and I knew I'd done something terrible, but I didn't know what it was and I couldn't move. Nanna kept shouting my name, over and over again. And when I didn't get the stone, Nanna said she'd get it for me, but she fell… and then I fell too.

Chapter 17

I woke up sweating; my duvet on the floor and the bottom sheet tangled round my body. It looked like I'd been ten rounds with a sumo wrestler, and lost. I tried to straighten the sheet and pulled the duvet back onto the bed, but it was too hot and I couldn't relax. My legs were twitchy and every time I closed my eyes, I felt sick.

Needing a drink of water, I got up, tiptoed across the hall and over to the bathroom. As I went to turn the handle, someone on the other side beat me to it and the door opened away from me.

"Oh!" Pearl jumped when she saw me. Even at night she wore her make-up. Except it was smudged and messy and her face was unnaturally green. "It's the frisbee cheating schizoid! Why are you creeping around like that?"

I found myself justifying what I was doing. "I didn't want to wake anyone," I said.

"Spare me," she said, her voice loaded with contempt. Then she grabbed my pyjama top, pulled me close and whispered, right into my face. "If you've been in my room, you're dead."

I shook myself free. "Get lost," I said, and pushed past her into the bathroom. My heart was actually racing, even though I wasn't scared of Pearl. I splashed my face with water, had a drink from my cupped hands and looked in the mirror. "I've got a witch mad at me and there is no way I am ever going to fit in here," I said.

Back in my room, I pulled out Lucy's book.

'Dear Lucy,' I wrote, but as hard as I tried, I couldn't think of a single thing to say.

I put down the pen, went over to the window and pushed it wide open. My bedroom was only on the first floor, but the drop was more than I could manage. I could see stars and the moon and the outline of hills in the distance. They were solid and still and I felt calmer looking at them. I had this crazy idea that the solution was out there in the hills, as far as away as possible. A place where there isn't any trouble. No more bad dreams, no more Pearl, no more me. I could reinvent myself and live happily ever after.

"You can't run away from problems," said the nanna in my head.

"Do what you damn well like, Ruby," said the dad.

I put on my trainers and grabbed my bag of stones.

"Everything changes. Things WILL get better," said Nanna.

"Oh and you'd know would you, Mrs Isn't-Life-Wonderful?" said Dad.

"You will go home, soon. There's no place like home…"

"Boil your head, Lucinda..."

"Can't you two just shut up for once?" I said, much too loudly. If Pearl was still awake, she would definitely have heard and everyone would know about it before morning. I couldn't take any more.

Holding my breath practically all the way, I tip-toed to the stairs and went down, gripping the hand rail to reduce my weight on the creaking steps. At the bottom, night staff clattered around in the kitchen, making cups of tea or midnight snacks, or maybe even setting up the breakfast. They couldn't have heard me above their noise, but I crept along, almost hugging the wall where the floorboards were most solid, and reached the entrance porch.

There was a door and a window. The window was narrow, but the door had a chain across and two bolts, high and low. I slid the chain easily and gently let it hang, then slipped the two bolts. When I pressed the handle down and pushed, the door stayed shut. I used both hands, pulling and pushing, but it wouldn't move. I needed a key.

My eyes scanned the hall, but my heart and brain both knew it was on somebody's belt along with all the other keys.

Just then, I heard another door. Someone coming out of the kitchen. I froze, wide-eyed, feeling my life whiz before me. Stupidly, I tried the front door again, as if it was going to suddenly miraculously open. The footsteps and laughter got nearer. I tried another door and it opened so I slipped in, closing it behind me as quietly as possible. I could have hidden under the desk or behind a sofa, but every step felt like an elephant thump. Inches away from me, separated only by the office door, someone fiddled with a bunch of keys.

"What would you do with a real brain if you had one, Ruby Garnett?" I whispered to myself, waiting and hoping that whoever it was didn't want to come in.

"Didn't you lock up? The chain's not on," called Tammy the night-awake, from the other side of the door. "It's not bolted either."

I held my breath.

Footsteps came out into the hall. "I came in the back way. Must have been Tom. I thought he'd locked up. What is he like eh? Best not let on..."

And then the door outside opened and I could hear footsteps on the gravel and the rubbish bins being pushed down to the gateway. Then footsteps back to the house and all the sounds of the door clunking shut, bolts and the chain slipping into place and then Tammy and Elaine gassing about whether there was enough rice crispies for breakfast and whether anyone actually liked cornflakes.

When it was totally silent again, I breathed.

I went over to Mrs Stein's window and pulled open one of the long velvet curtains hoping to find another escape route. But instead of freedom, there were wooden shutters, bolted at the top and bottom and typically, a tiny padlock held each lower bolt in place. I tried the next window, and the next, but they were all the same.

Back in my room, I sat on the floor and quietly tipped the stones out of my bag. I started to arrange them in a line, the biggest rock next to my bed, winding down to the smallest pebble of all. Singing "Follow the Ruby brick road, follow the Ruby brick road," I used all the stones, and the little path was almost out of the door.

Chapter 18

While I was eating breakfast, Lily gave me another letter from my mum. She also gave letters to Amy and Bianca who ripped them open at once. I put my letter next to my plate and polished off four slices of buttery toast and jam, before I even thought about opening mine.

"Aren't you going to read it?" said Pearl.

"What's it to you?" I said.

"Nothing," she said, shrugging.

Bianca put her letter back in the envelope.

"Who's that from then?" said Pearl.

"My cousin. She's got her picture in the paper."

"Show me," said Pearl.

Bianca took out a newspaper clipping and a piece of paper with a child's handwriting on it. I couldn't read what it said.

"That's not a proper letter," said Pearl.

"It is," said Bianca. "Just cos you never get anything…"

I looked down at my envelope. Mum had drawn little flowers in the corner and put a tiny little love heart next to my name, but I still didn't open it.

Back in my room, I threw the letter onto my bed. "I'm not reading you," I said. "Love hearts or not." Then I brushed my teeth, pulled on my hoody and grabbed my school stuff.

Outside, Pearl and Bianca were still arguing. I put my ear to the door and listened. I didn't want to go out there in the middle of a shouting match.

"A proper letter's got news and stuff. That's just a stupid photo torn out of a newspaper," said Pearl.

"At least I got something," said Bianca.

I looked again at my letter. I don't have to do this, I thought, picking it up, lifting the sticky flap and pulling out the paper. I'm only checking for photos of Lucy. And then before I knew it, Mum's words were staring back at me.

Dear Ruby,

I'm sad you haven't written to me, but I won't give up trying. I do understand how you feel. At least, I think I do. But we should talk.

I am still being a stay-at-home mum and allowing myself to enjoy it. I've got some work, baking for a local café and I can do that in the evenings when Lucy is in bed. When you come home, I'll rethink that one. You girls are my priority now.

Lucy is growing by the day and there are definitely some teeth on the verge of popping through. She dribbles all the time. Silver Bells, Nanna used to call it. She also makes lots of different sounds and I like to think she is learning to talk. My only disappointment is that you are not here with us. I show Lucy pictures of you every day, so that she remembers you when we see you.

I would love to visit. What do you say? PLEASE reply. It doesn't have to be very much.

Love you always,
Mum xxx

It was the stuff about Lucy which got me.

The day Mum went into labour we were in ASDA, buying baby things. We didn't know if Lucy would be a boy or a girl and we were arguing about buying yellow or blue sleep suits.

Mum was being crabby and she kept stopping and holding her stomach. She said it was just a tummy ache, then she practically shouted at me, "It doesn't bloody matter what colour sleep suits it has! Just grab one and pay, so we can get out of here."

I took her purse, but by the time I had been through the checkout, Mum's waters had broken, which meant the baby was on its way.

The lady on the help desk called an ambulance. I knew what to do. I knew about how Mum had to do special breathing and about rubbing her back to stop it hurting and keeping calm, but the ASDA lady took charge and said, "We'll make sure she's looked after." She wouldn't let me get in the ambulance, and I didn't want another argument and make it difficult for Mum when she already had enough to worry about. I wanted Mum to say "No, she's coming with me," like we'd planned. But she didn't. She didn't say a thing.

I watched the ambulance drive away with Mum inside and the lady from ASDA looking all smug, and then Mrs Scott came to fetch me. By the time we got to the hospital, Lucy was born and lying asleep on Mum's belly, in a sort of pink nightie and a throw away nappy.

I stopped in the doorway and stared at my baby sister. Mum smiled at me, then nodded, so I went over and picked Lucy up into my arms. I wanted to be cross with Mum for leaving me behind, but when I saw Lucy I couldn't be cross even if I tried. I stared at her tiny curled up fingers and adorable little feet, her perfect baby ears and squashed nose. I watched her blue eyes open for the very first time, even before Mum, before anyone, and my smile lifted me into the air. In those precious minutes, even though Nanna wasn't there, the world was perfect. I called her Lucy, after Nanna.

The memory of Lucy's birth made me feel happy and sad at the same time. I had wanted a sister all my life, and now that I had one, the idea that she might forget me was unthinkable. So I tore a piece of paper out of my book, and wrote,

Dear Mum,
Yes, come and visit. And bring Lucy.
Ruby

I folded the paper and stuffed it back into the envelope, taping it closed with the sellotape Lily had left in my room. I scribbled out my name and the High Fell Hall address, and wrote Mum's name and address instead.

Before I went across to school, I found Lily and asked her to post it for me.

Chapter 19

When I went for my weekly meeting with Danielle, the door was closed. I turned the handle very quietly and peered into the room. Danielle had her back to me, but opposite her was Pearl. From where I stood, it looked like Pearl was hitting something on the table in front of her. And when I say hitting, I mean beating whatever it was. To death. I'd seen Pearl angry, I'd even been on the receiving end of her blows, but in that moment of wide eyes, clenched teeth and monster grunting, ANGRY was an understatement.

I couldn't take my eyes off her and she was way too mad to notice me.

She shouted, "Why?" and then lobbed something across the room, thwacking it against the wall.

"Doesn't."

Thwack.

"Anyone."

Thwack.

"Want."

Thwack.

"Me?"

I thought she had seen me, but she didn't leap up or try to kill me or even slam the door shut. She just carried on banging the table and throwing things at the wall.

Thwack thwack thwack.

I shut the door, and stood there for a minute half expecting her to open it again and pulp me for invading her private moment. When she didn't, I sat down on Danielle's step, listening to Pearl's grunts, and the dull thuds on the wall behind me.

I was still leaning on the door when it opened, and I fell in.

"Oh, Ruby!" said Danielle. "You're here."

I stood up, trying to look past Danielle into the room. "Am I early?" I said.

Danielle checked her watch. "I'm afraid we've overrun a little, so I'm not quite ready. Would you like to come back in ten minutes?"

I didn't get a chance to answer before Pearl appeared behind Danielle. "I'm all right," she said. "I'm going now anyway." Her black and green make-up was streaked across her cheeks, despite the obvious attempt to wipe it off. She looked right at me. "Your turn!" she said, with a fake cheerful voice. "Have fun!"

"I don't want you to leave just yet," said Danielle.

"And I don't want to stay," said Pearl.

I felt guilty for seeing her like that and I heard myself say, "I'm sorry."

"Yeah, me too," she said.

Our eyes met then, just for like, a second and I felt terribly, terribly sad. Behind all that anger and smudged make-up, she had the same baby blue eyes as my sister Lucy, and I felt strangely close to her.

Pearl nodded. "Thanks," she said, then pushed past, knocking me off the step, and disappearing into the house. Danielle followed, so I sat back down on the step and waited for her to return.

Once Danielle had cleaned up, I was allowed to go in. There were leftover bits of grey clay on the walls. The table was still damp from where it had been washed, but otherwise everything was normal. Danielle said to me, "It was nice to hear you two apologise, especially after all this time."

I shrugged.

"How are you getting along now?"

Another shrug. "We're not," I said, and went over to the bag of clay. "Can I use this?" Without waiting for an answer, I tipped it onto the table Danielle had just cleaned. "What shall I make?" I said.

"What do you want to make?"

"What did Pearl make?"

Danielle's eyes narrowed and she sat up slightly. "Were you listening?" she said.

My neck went hot, and then my face. I must have turned flamingo pink. I said, "No! Honest. The clay was out and Pearl was here before me. I just assumed."

Danielle didn't say anything.

I dipped my hands in the water and then rubbed them all over the ball of clay. It went slimy and muddy and I dug my fingers deep inside the squidgy lump, then started pulling little chunks off and rolling them into baby pebble shapes. "What did Pearl do with the clay?" Obviously I knew. I just wanted to know more.

Danielle didn't answer me.

I lined up the little clay balls in a row along the edge of the table, but all the while I couldn't stop thinking about Pearl. "Does she come and see you every week?" I said, because I had never seen her there before.

"Are we still talking about Pearl?" said Danielle.

"What does SHE do when she's here?"

"Ruby, I'm happy for YOU to talk to me about the other girls, and how it affects YOU, but I'M not going to talk about them."

I looked at the little clay balls sitting happily in a nice straight line, and I was tempted to throw them against the wall, to see what it felt like. I picked one up, weighed it in my hand and took aim. Danielle sat back in her chair, out of the way. Except that when it came to it, I couldn't really be bothered, and instead, I SLAMMED my fist down on top of each little ball; one by one until they were all squished flat.

"Just tell me one thing," I said. "Does she have ANY family?" Because if she did, she was so obviously a proper gigantic drama queen and I didn't need to feel sorry for her. I didn't want to feel sorry for her. I especially didn't want to find reasons to like her.

Danielle said. "If you want to know about Pearl, why don't you ask her yourself?"

Like that's going to happen.

I didn't ask any more questions because Danielle was so obviously NOT going to tell me anything. Instead, I rolled up all the clay into one giant confusing ball again, and ignored her.

Chapter 20

The next week, Mum spoke to Mrs Stein and they made a plan. The plan was that she would get the train up and we would meet her at Morecambe Station, then me and Mum and Lucy would spend some time in Morecambe together, before going back to school.

Tom took me to the station in the mini-bus and I was so excited I could have burst! I couldn't wait to cuddle my little squidgy sister and see how much she had grown and teach her to say Ruby and clap her hands and maybe even walk. But most of all, I wanted to say sorry. Even if she didn't understand it, I wanted to say sorry for leaving her.

At the station, a whole family of butterflies danced in my tummy, and when the train pulled in they went crazy, twisting, waltzing and doing the tango. The train stopped, doors opened and lots of people started getting off, but I saw Mum straight away. I waited for her to turn around and get the buggy off the train. Except that she didn't. She started walking towards me. ALONE.

Don't forget Lucy, I thought. But Mum just kept walking towards me, smiling.

"MUM! Where's Lucy?" I shouted.

Her smile dropped and there was like, this eternal moment of staring at each other, butterflies dead in my guts. Then the guard whistled and the doors closed and the train pulled out of the station.

Tom said, "That has to be your mum," and he held my arm and walked me up the platform.

Mum stood there shaking her head, watching us, and then suddenly she burst into a big smile and laughed out loud. "Oh my god, Ruby, look at you," she said. "You are a picture."

"Where's Lucy?"

Mum's face screwed up. "I'm sorry…" she started to say.

"But you said..."

She shook her head. "I didn't say anything, Ruby."

"But why didn't you bring her? Is she all right? Is she ill?"

Mum looked at Tom and he looked at the ground. "I wanted it to be just US," said Mum. "Lucy's spending the day with Mrs Scott. They are very fond of each other."

"But she's my sister. I wanted to see her. You know I wanted to see her." And I couldn't help thinking that Mum didn't trust me and this was some kind of punishment for leaving Lucy before.

"Let me hug you," said Mum, ignoring my upset and grabbing me before I could protest. I didn't hug her back though, just stood there with my arms down by my sides, looking out towards the sea.

"You're still angry with me," she said, standing back.

I thought, first Dad, now Lucy. When would she ever listen to what I wanted? "Yes, I'm angry," I said.

"Oh baby," she said, and stroked my cheek.

I brushed her hand away. "I'm not a baby," I said.

"I'm sorry. I was only…"

I butted in. "If you're so desperate to stroke baby cheeks, you should have brought Lucy."

Mum held her hands up. "You're right. I'm sorry. I promise faithfully, next time, I will bring Lucy."

Tom looked at his watch and said, "Is that the time? I'd better be going back to school." He gave Mum a phone number for emergencies and said he would come back at three to take us to High Fell. We watched in silence while Tom walked back up the platform and out to the car park.

When Tom was out of sight, Mum said, "Friends?"

She put her arms around me and tried to hug me again.

"Have you stopped smoking?" I said, because she didn't smell of smoke.

"Yes I have," she said, proudly. "It's all part of the new me." She patted her hair. "What do you think?"

"Oh, you've dyed your hair again," I said. It was bright orange this time.

"Henna," she said. It's more natural. Do you like it?"

"I can smell perfume," I said, refusing to agree that the new hair did actually suit her.

She lifted her wrist to my nose. "It's Pure Purple. It represents freedom and independence. That's the new me."

"Freedom and independence eh?" I said, because I'd heard it all before.

When Dad had work trips he was always vague about where he was going. Mum hated it. "You could just give me an address, in case of emergency," she'd beg, and Dad would say, "But what will my colleagues think when you're checking up on me every five minutes?" And then he'd leave and Mum would be all huffy and say things like, "Yeah, well I can do independent too. Just watch me." And then he'd come back and I'd find him eating breakfast, laughing and joking and handing out compliments to everyone as if we were the happiest family alive.

Mum smiled. Her face had more lines than it used to. She looked like Nanna. "Yes, independent. And I'm going to a better Me, an honest Me, a Me who takes time to listen to her daughters."

I looked down at my feet, trying to work out if I was being mean to her.

"Even when they're not speaking," added Mum. She held her arms open for me again. It would have been so easy to just hug her back and forget everything. "Help me out, Ruby. I'm doing my best here."

"What about Dad?"

Her arms dropped and she sighed. "Loose ends, Ruby. We tied up some loose ends. Money stuff, that's all."

When I was little, I wanted to believe in Father Christmas, the Easter Bunny and the Tooth Fairy. Just like I wanted to believe in my mum. But once you know they're not for real, you can never go back; not without proof.

I told Mum I was hungry, so we found a café where I ate jam scones and hot chocolate and Mum put sweeteners in her black coffee. We looked out of the big bay windows at the sea. This wasn't how I planned it. I was supposed to be huggling Lucy and having a good time with her, not sitting in gloomy silence with Mum.

Mum scratched at some jam I had spilled on the table cloth. "Rube?" she said, wiping her jammy nail on a paper napkin. She didn't look at me.

"What?"

Then she started collecting my scone crumbs together in a pile.

"What?" I said.

She brushed them into her hand and dropped them on the plate with the jam napkin and took a deep breath before she spoke. "I... I've put in for a house swap," she stammered. "Do... do you mind?"

Mind? It was a relief. Like, my body literally relaxed. Going back to the same place where it had all happened was the last thing I wanted to do. I didn't want to remember anything about that day. "How long will it take?"

Mum looked up. "I don't know. That depends on who wants to swap with us. Do you mind? Only, do say. Do say if you don't want to. I... I just thought... you know..."

I smiled at her then, probably my first smile all day. If we moved, he wouldn't know where we were. "No, I don't mind. I want to move. Honest."

Mum reached across the crumb-less and jam free tablecloth to hold my hand. This time, I didn't pull away.

Before she paid the bill, Mum took some pictures out of her purse. They were pictures of Mum with Lucy on her lap, taken in a passport photo machine. "We had these taken especially for you to keep." Mum was getting Lucy to wave and they were obviously both laughing. Lucy had changed so much since that night I left her.

"Can she say anything yet?"

"It's mostly babble, but she thinks she's talking," said Mum.

"Can she stand? Can she crawl? What does she do?"

Mum laughed. "Come on, let's walk and talk at the same time."

Chapter 21

Morecambe prom is a proper seaside place with lots of amusements and fish and chip shops and fortune tellers, but there's also an amazing view stretching away across the bay to the Lake District hills. They were slightly hazy in the summer sun, and that made them look distant and mysterious.

"My school's over there, in those hills," I told Mum, almost proudly. Tom had pointed this out to me on the way down in the mini-bus.

Another nice thing about Morecambe was the crazy bird sculptures. All along the prom were statues and models of birds, standing on bollards, flocks of them in flight; stuck to fences, standing on rocks, sitting on the ground, in the middle of roundabouts. Sea birds. I loved them. Nanna would have loved them too. Mum said they were weird, but in a good way. We walked up and down and Mum took pictures on her mobile phone of me, the sculptures, me and the sculptures, the sculptures with me behind, in front and next to… and so on.

And then Mum said, "I want to buy you something."

"No, its okay," I said, knowing full well she didn't have money to waste on things I didn't need. But when we found an indoor market, Mum marched me inside.

My eyes danced around the stalls and landed on one selling wicked Converse in just about any colour you could imagine. Mum must have seen them too. "Come on," she said. "It's about time I treated you."

The boots were twenty pounds which was cheap compared to other places, but when Mum opened her purse she only had two twenty-pound-notes and some loose change left. If she spent half her money on me, she might not have enough left to get home. I thought about all the times I took money from Nanna's purse and all the times Nanna laughed about money being like water, and her purse being like a leaky tap. She must have known. She must have suspected something. I wanted to confess everything.

"What's your favourite colour?" Mum asked. The boots were arranged in a rainbow of colours on top of their little boxes.

"Can I tell you something?"

"Now don't try and pretend you don't want any because I saw the way you looked at them," said Mum.

"But I really don't," I insisted. There were more important things on my mind.

"It's called denial, you know; where you insist something is one way, when on some other level, you KNOW it isn't. Trust me, I'm an expert. And anyway, I shall be very disappointed if I can't buy you a present. You deserve something special." She picked up the red ones. "Oh look!" she said. "Ruby slippers! You should have these."

In the Wizard of Oz, Dorothy wears ruby slippers and when she gets homesick, she just has to tap her heels together three times and say "there's no place like home," and everything is all right. It was the most famous line in the whole film, but I didn't know Mum knew it. "How do you know?"

"She was your nanna, but she was my mum. I was brought up on that film too. And we did talk you know. She loved that you cherished it as much as she did."

That gave me a warm feeling. It was a link to Nanna I wasn't expecting; and I guess a link to Mum too.

Mum paid for the red shoes and I tucked them into my backpack along with my stones and when we left the market, I tucked my arm into Mum's and gave her a little squeeze.

"I bet you're hungry again aren't you?" said Mum. "Fish and chips?"

"Thank you," I said.

"You don't have to thank me. All this fresh sea air is making me hungry too."

"I mean thank you for … well, for being here. For the ruby slippers. For… you know." Mum wasn't so bad. She was really making an effort. Maybe she had changed for good this time.

We sat on the beach with our fish and chips in polystyrene trays and ate them with bendy plastic forks. I wanted the moment to last forever. No more going back to school, no more going back to our house, no more Dad.

When Mum had eaten every last scrap she kicked off her shoes and lay back in the sand. "We used to do this when I was a kid," she said. "Fish and chips out of the paper, the smell of vinegar, the sound of seagulls overhead, the feel of sand between your toes. Life doesn't get any…"

"…better than this!" I finished for her. "Nanna said that to me too."

Mum sat up and looked straight at me. "You miss her more than anyone," she said. "Can we talk, Ruby?"

Not now, I pleaded silently. "Look at the clouds," I said. "I can see a face in that one..."

"There's something you should know."

"…an old man with a beard," I said, pointing.

Mum grabbed my arm from out of the sky, and held my hand in hers. She spoke slowly, straight into my face. "It wasn't. Your. Fault."

Easy for her to say. She wasn't there.

I shook my hand free and looked down the beach towards the stone jetty. There were three bird statues on a rock, big and black with their wings open. I knew they were cormorants. I saw some on a river once when I was with Nanna.

"Ruby, nobody blames you. She wasn't well…" Mum started to say.

"I'm not listening," I said, and jumped up before she could stop me, scattering my left over fish and chips on the beach for the gulls. "Let's find some treasure for Lucy instead." I picked up shells for my sister and the prettiest pebbles to add to my collection.

When Mum joined me, she started collecting too and before long, we were both overloaded. She laughed. Then I laughed; not big split-your-sides kind of laughter, just chuckles and giggles.

And then, past the stone jetty I found a rock with a shell pattern pressed into it.

"A fossil!" said Mum, like she'd discovered buried treasure.

I'd never seen a fossil in real life, only ever in a museum. "It's millions of years old," I said, trying to imagine that far back.

"Squillions," said Mum.

"Zillions," I said. And then I wondered how far back you could actually go, because everything starts somewhere. "How DID the world begin?" I asked.

Mum rolled her eyes. "Magic?"

Magic is for kids. It's not real. "I don't believe in magic any more," I said.

"Oh!" said Mum. She looked disappointed, maybe even surprised. There was still a gigantic gap between us, and in it was all the stuff she didn't know about me, and all the stuff I didn't know about her. "Well in that case, it's science. You do believe in science don't you?" She reached across the empty space and held my hand.

"Tell me about it," I said.

We sat down on the sand. "Once upon a time there was nothing," said Mum. "And then there was a build up of pressure, or something, and a big explosion. Bang! Rocks and gases and debris, flew out in all directions. That's when all the stars were made, and then all the planets... and then gradually, somehow, life evolved..." She shrugged. "And here we are. You and me on Morecambe beach, at the beginning of the world."

I held onto her arm and rested my head on her shoulder.

"I love you, Ruby Garnett," she said.

Chapter 22

Tom came to collect us in a car, and Mum and I sat in the back together. I surprised myself to be glad that Lucy hadn't come. Mum would have had to think about where to feed and change her, and it would have got in the way of everything we did. It was like those weeks before Lucy was born, being on my own with Mum and discovering that we liked each other after all.

Mum kept looking at me and smiling all the way back to school, and when we reached the drive, she said, "I can't wait to meet all your friends."

When I was in junior school, I used to have a friend called Sophia. Sophia had never had a nightmare, she always wore clean white socks and ironed clothes and she wasn't allowed to get her ears pierced, in case she regretted it later. I used to go to her house for tea and sometimes she'd come to mine. Nanna would cook us something really special, like spag bol or kiev, and then we'd watch telly before Sophia's mum came to collect her. I tried not to invite her when Dad was home, because of his embarrassing jokes which weren't at all funny, but sometimes he'd turn up, unexpected.

The last time Sophia came, Dad arrived just as Nanna was serving our tea so he sat and ate with us, drank nearly a whole bottle of wine and got all mushy and embarrassing about how it was so good to have friends and how happy he was that I had Sophia. I wanted to die, and Nanna must have counted to ten about a hundred times. When Sophia's mum arrived to collect her, my dad went to the door and said how charming Sophia was, and how beautiful she (the mum) was, complimenting her clothes and her hair and calling her Gina after every sentence. I suppose he was trying to be polite, but his breath smelled of booze, his speech was slurred and his 'winning' smile was boss-eyed. Sophia never came to my house again.

When I moved into secondary school, I made friends with Courtney. Courtney's favourite lesson was drama and we liked the same TV programmes so I invited her home to watch my Oz DVD. I told her it was a about a girl who lives with her boring family in dull brown Kansas, and how she gets blown to Oz and meets all these crazy colourful people and witches and munchkins and has to find this wizard to make everything right. I even thought we might be able to act out the scenes together, or do it in drama. I was so excited. And Courtney brought round Doritos and dips and Nanna made us knickerbocker glories and for just a few minutes, life was wonderful.

I put the film on and Courtney said, "It's black and white!"

"Don't worry, it changes," I said.

"But it's dead old," said Courtney. "I thought it was gonna be like Harry Potter."

And then Dad arrived home smelling of booze - like he had some kind of freaky psychic knowledge about when I had company - and joined in. "You're not watching this rubbish again are you?"

"I hate old films!" said Courtney.

"Course you do. But she's not normal," he said, nodding at me. "Sits in her room and pretends she's IN the bloody film!"

"You never do!" said Courtney.

"Sings to herself in front of the mirror and everything," said Dad.

"No way," said Courtney.

…And on and on they went. The two of them making out I was some kind of mental lunatic and ganging up on me. In school, Courtney told everyone and we fell out.

I never invited anyone home again after that; not that they would have come.

So apart from when I was really little at playgroup and first school, Mum had NEVER met a single friend of mine, and I didn't want to spoil the day by telling her I didn't have any. Instead, I showed her round the house and the garden and then took her up to my room.

She sat on my bed and said, "You will make the most of this opportunity won't you, Ruby?"

I was on the floor with my new fossil and my old collection of stones, grading them in order of loveliness and I didn't answer.

"Ruby?"

I shrugged. High Fell Hall wasn't an opportunity; it was a sentence.

"Because I want you to come home sooner rather than later. I want us to be a family," said Mum. "Just us girls."

I thought about Mum and Lucy and me cosying up on the sofa, reading Lucy stories and drinking hot chocolate before bedtime. But then Dad slipped into my daydream and a shiver went down the back of my neck.

"Mum?" I had to ask.

"Yes?"

"Would you let him back again?"

Mum shook her head. "No. Not again. He's walked out on us one too many times. He won't be coming back to live with us."

The definiteness in her voice felt good, but there was still one thing which didn't add up. "Why did you get all dressed up to meet him?"

"For me," she said. "Not for him. Because I hadn't been anywhere since Lucy was born. I just wanted to look nice. That's all."

I wanted to believe her.

"Ruby, he phoned me. I told him not to set foot in the house ever again. He asked me to meet him, to talk about it. I said no, at first. But then he said he could help us out with money. That's why I met him. Except of course, it was all hot air. Just another one of the things he says, and doesn't mean. After all these years, I fell for it."

"Did you go to Les Amants?"

"No, we did not," she said. "I arrived at the Eastern Tandoori and saw it was closed, and he turned up. He didn't say he'd rung home, or I would have known you'd be upset. He wanted to go to Les Amants, but our days of candlelit dinners are long gone and I point blank refused. We walked around a while and ended up in MacDonald's…" Mum hated Macdonald's.

"Why there?"

"Because it's well lit and I knew I'd end up paying." Mum looked embarrassed. "And before you ask, the BIG PLAN to help us financially involved signing my life away to underwrite some dodgy loan for him." She shook her head. "And that isn't going to happen."

I didn't know what to say.

"It's taken me a long time to realise this, Ruby, but he isn't interested in us. He didn't even ask about Lucy. He's never even met her; his own daughter! No, he's only interested in number one. Him."

I felt guilty. "I'm sorry I didn't trust you," I said.

Mum shook her head. "I don't blame you. Honestly. But we're friends again and that's all that matters."

"Can't I just come home now?" I said, impatient for my new life to begin. "I'm better. I promise I won't leave Lucy again or jump into shop windows or mess up at school." I didn't plan to say it, and before I met Mum in Morecambe, happy families were the last thing on my brain.

Mum looked down at the floor. "It's not up to me," she mumbled. "They have to be sure, you know, that you won't do anything daft again."

"But I won't."

"I believe you."

"But they don't?"

"You need to talk, Ruby. You need to talk about everything that's happened."

"Why? What's the point? It's all in the past."

"Because it will help to get you better. And it will help to get you home…"

There was a knock at my door which I would happily have ignored, but Mum stood up and opened it.

There was Pearl, chewing gum. "I've been told to ask if you want tea."

Mum looked at me. "Is that all right?"

I nodded.

"Thank you," she said to Pearl. "Are you one of Ruby's friends? I do like the way you've done your face." She was obviously trying to be cool, and down with the kids, and when Pearl laughed out loud, Mum invited her in.

"No, I'm all right," she said. "It's really kind of you. Got stuff to do though…"

But Mum wouldn't let Pearl go. She asked where she was from. Pearl was from Bexleyheath, not a million miles from our home in Sidcup. Mum asked how long she'd been at High Fell and Pearl came out with her story about foster carers being a bit thin on the ground and not having anywhere else to go.

I was grateful to Pearl, because she made it look like I had at least got one friend, and when she turned to go I smiled and sort of nodded my thanks at her. Pearl just seemed to find the whole thing utterly amusing.

When Mum left, I felt empty and sad. I thought a lot about how my life had changed since Nanna had gone, but how I still had a family and things to look forward to. And then I thought about Pearl all alone in the world, and that made me sad too. I didn't expect it to, but it did.

My eye lids were getting heavy and yet I didn't want to go to sleep. Outside it was dark and there was no moon and no stars. From the comfort of my bed, I could just about make out the ceiling and imagined a beautiful night sky where the moon was bright and stars twinkled. I thought about my nanna and wondered where she was in all that darkness. I saw a shooting star and had a wish that one day my life would be nice, and normal, and I'd be home with my sister. Then I imagined that shooting star exploding into a million little pieces just like really happened when the world started, squillions of years ago. And then it all went dark and there was nothing.

Chapter 23

I took my backpack off and got out the fossil from the front pocket, where it was specially wrapped in Kleenex to keep it from getting scratched. I gave it to Danielle. She held the fossil in its little tissue nest and traced the lines of the shell mark with her finger tips.

"Where did you find it?"

"Morecambe beach, when I met my mum."

"Ah yes, your mum," she said. "And how was that?"

I stood up and went over to the cupboards. There was a ridiculous smile hovering around my mouth which I didn't want Danielle to see. My happy feeling was still fragile. Like a party balloon, it might burst, or drift away forever if I had to share it, so I didn't answer. Instead I floated around the games, looking for something which didn't need me to concentrate.

"You don't want to tell me about your day with Mum," said Danielle.

I shrugged.

When my amethyst disappeared, Nanna took me to a gemstone market in London. I was a kid in a sweet shop, wanting everything, from the pretty polished stones to the beautiful and expensive crystals. Nanna told me they were over-the-rainbow-diamonds, because when the light was right you could see all the colours of the spectrum in angles of the glass. I was allowed to choose whichever stone I wanted, and of course I went straight to the amethysts. They were all a rich deep purple and cut into tear-drop shapes; dazzling and beautiful, but too refined and perfect for me. The stall keeper asked my name. He laughed when I told him it was Ruby Garnett. He said, "Ruby, Ruby, Ruby, the most precious of them all." And he showed me his ring, a lovely red ruby, surrounded by diamonds set in a golden clasp. I thought, one day I'm going to have a precious ruby just like that.

When I got home, I showed Mum the tiny pieces of speckled bloodstone and red coral I had chosen. I was happy, excited, and fit to burst telling her about the choice I'd had and the amazing over-the-rainbow-diamonds and the ruby ring... But all she said was, "That low-life took your amethyst."

So even though things were different now, I knew all about balloons bursting and the need to keep the good stuff private.

I picked up a pack of cards, and said, "Snap?" because it was mindless and simple. Danielle didn't complain. She had the easiest job in the world, playing games with a thirteen year old. I could have done anything and she would have let me. While I dealt the cards I asked her, "What is the point of me being here?"

"Here? As in this room with me, or as in school?"

"Both," I said.

Danielle was quiet for a few seconds and then said, "You've had some pretty traumatic events to deal with in your life Ruby, and you're here at school to give you a bit of breathing space. Time with me is just special time; a chance for you to remember and explore some of those events and your feelings about them, if you want to. My job is to facilitate that."

I wanted to say well you're not doing it very well, because she practically never asked me anything and she didn't have any idea how I felt. But being there was better than being most places so I kept my mouth shut and put down a card.

Danielle went next, laying the three of spades on top of my card.

Me, her, me, her. Backward and forwards.

Two of spades.

Four of diamonds.

Jack of hearts.

King of clubs. He had my dad's black curly hair falling all over his shoulders.

Queen of Hearts. The one with the saddest eyes.

Seven of diamonds.

Seven of spades.

"SNAP!" shouted Danielle, slamming her hand on the top card.

I flinched. In my head, there was the flash of a memory. Dad and Nanna. I didn't even notice the snap.

Danielle collected her winning pile. It was my turn to start. "Concentrate, Ruby," I said, trying to block any more ugly memories jumping into my brain.

Queen of Diamonds.

King of Diamonds…

And so on.

It was all so much easier than talking. Except that I couldn't stop thinking about HIM.

That first time he left, he went off with another woman. My mum found pictures of her in his jacket, which was utterly stupid and indiscreet of him. I never saw the pictures because Mum tore them up and set fire to them in her ashtray. Then she chain smoked on the sofa and didn't move until Dad came home. I was sent to Nanna's while they DISCUSSED it. When I came home, Dad was gone. Mum said he'd gone to the off-license but he never came back.

My biggest memory of that time is of Mum, spending hours in front of the mirror, being totally obsessed by the way she looked and yet always ending up with red eyes, smudged lipstick and a ragged bob. She missed work, didn't eat and I don't suppose she slept very much. She didn't notice how upset I was. She was a mess. We were both a mess.

And then one day, Dad came home again.

I don't know what happened to the other woman, but when Dad came back, he wasn't the same. It was as if he'd left a piece of himself behind and he never even pretended to be nice or funny or crazy any more. He was unpredictable and moody. There were arguments about how much money he drank away and arguments about who'd been searching his pockets, and arguments about having to account for himself because he was a 'GROWN MAN'. And when Nanna took me out, away from it all, he was like Mr PARANOIA when I came back. "What did she say about me? What did you tell her? She doesn't like me, does she?

"Snap," said Danielle, again.

I looked down at the cards and she was right. Two fours. With the back of my arm, I swept the cards onto the floor.

Danielle sat back in her chair and said, "You're angry."

"State the obvious why don't you," I said. I hated the way she looked over the top of her glasses when she spoke, and that she was just so unbothered about me being clearly upset.

"Do you want to tell me what you're angry about?" she said, all calm and unruffled

And I thought, do you want me to write a list? Because what with them keeping me at High Fell against my will, and what with Danielle always managing to dredge up some nasty memory, and what with everyone hating me, and my nanna being dead, and my sister probably not even recognising me when I eventually got see her, my anger shouldn't have come as a surprise to anyone. For about a millisecond, I was tempted to get out a pen and paper, write it all down and pin it on the wall. But I didn't.

I picked up my bag, threw it over my shoulder and walked out.

Chapter 24

I stormed through the house, slamming doors and ignoring everyone in my path. I didn't give a damn about the noise or the cracked plaster or the visitors in the big room, and I charged up the stairs two at a time.

The door to my own room was blocked by Pearl, piles of books, old clothes and screwed up bits of rubbish.

"And WHAT do you think YOU'RE doing?" I demanded.

Pearl pulled a black bin liner away from my door. "Sorry," she said, looking at the ground.

There was enough room for me to get through, but Pearl's stuff was just a foot-tempting kick away and she wasn't even looking.

But then she did. "I need to get rid of some stuff if anyone's going to want me," she said, in an embarrassed, half joking half serious, kind of way. And her eyes were red, as in a just-been-crying kind of a way.

"Of course someone will want you," I said, impatiently. I certainly didn't mean it to sound nice. It was just one of those contrary moments I suppose, but Pearl smiled a fantastically grateful smile and I got one of those I'm-a-nice-person feelings. My urge to kick Pearl's stuff just melted.

"If there's anything you want, help yourself," she said.

I looked at the heap of junk. The clothes were never going to get below the WOULDN'T BE SEEN DEAD IN THAT radar, but there were lots of books, and I did like books. I moved a couple with my foot, and Pearl cleared a bigger space.

"Are you all right?" she said. I took off my backpack and parked my bum next to hers. "You look really fed up."

I grunted, "Danielle," as if that explained anything.

And Pearl said, "Oh. I see," like she really did.

There were dozens of paperbacks and hardbacks in two piles. "I'm keeping these," she said pointing to the small pile. "You can have any of those." And with her other hand she pointed at the larger pile. She wasn't wearing her glove. I'd never seen her glove-less before, and I couldn't help looking at her hand. It was wrinkly and smooth all at the same time, like her skin had been stretched out and then scrunched up again. She saw me looking, and I wanted her to explain why it was like that, without me having to ask. But she didn't. She just shifted her bum and turned slightly away from me so I couldn't see her hand any more.

I looked back at the unwanted pile of books. Mostly they were falling apart and too babyish for me, but then I saw a book I knew; 'THE WORLD OF CREATION STORY BOOK', in shiny FULL COLOUR! "Oh my god, I used to have exactly this book!" I said. "I loved it!"

Pearl smiled at me AGAIN. "Yeah, it was one of my favourites."

"Then why are you getting rid of it?" I would never get rid of anything that precious. When I was a kid, too many of my things just went missing and I never saw them again and it made me want to hang on to everything I loved. 'The World of Creation Story Book' was one of those things.

"Don't suppose I'll ever read it again," she said. "It's too young."

I started flicking through the pages and it all came to back to me; the pictures, the words, and even the smell of the paper reminded me of happy times when I stayed over at Nanna's and she read to me before bedtime. I knew the stories practically back to front. "Pangu! I used to love that one," I said, pouncing on a story from China. "His eyes were the sun and the moon…"

"And his teeth were made of stones," laughed Pearl, beside me.

"Oh my god! Nanna used to put her teeth in a glass at night," I said. "And I used to think they looked like tiny little stones all stuck in a pink rock..."

Mrs Stein came upstairs looking for me then. I thought she was going to tell me off for door slamming and other minor offences I may have committed, but she gave me a letter, which was obviously from my mum. She didn't even mention the other stuff. I shoved it into the front pocket of my bag, looked down at my book and expected her to go away. But she stood there NOT going away, hovering, like a hungry buzzard.

"What are you reading?" said Mrs Stein.

I passed the book up to her and as I did, a piece of creased but flattened paper fell out. I picked it up and was about to hand it to Pearl when I saw the writing. It said:

Eggs
Flour
Icing Sugar
Butter
Choc Vermicelli
Choc buttons

in curly, old-lady-writing. Exactly like Nanna's writing. A cold tingle ran down my back and made me shiver.

"Where did you get this?" I said.

"It was in the book. I think it came from a jumble sale. I kept it because it reminded me of the days when I used to bake cakes with my mum – they're all cake ingredients…"

"I know what they are," I snapped.

"All right, all right. I was just saying," said Pearl. "What's the big deal?"

I stared at the list, with the writing up close to my face. Could it be Nanna's writing? Could it be my book? "I used to have the same book," I said.

"Yes, you said"

"And my nanna used to read it to me."

"So?"

"And that list… it's like, her exact writing. It's almost as if she wrote it, as if that really is my book."

Mrs Stein was listening and gave me back the book. "I imagine a lot of people use shopping lists as book marks," she said.

"And train tickets," said Pearl. "And scratch cards and betting slips and I even heard of someone using a slice of bacon! Do you think that's true?"

Mrs Stein and Pearl laughed. They seemed to think it was very funny, but I felt like I was looking at a ghost and that wasn't funny at all. I tried to think. How could my book, with Nanna's shopping list inside, end up belonging to Pearl?

"Where exactly did you get this?" I said.

"I told you," said Pearl. "A jumble sale. At least, I think that's where it came from because my dad gave it to me and it was obviously *used*," she said, using air quotes. "He was a bit of a cheapskate like that."

I touched the writing with my finger tips. I really wanted the book to be mine; it would have been like finding an old friend. But as if? I mean, how could that possibly work? I passed the book and the list to Pearl.

"You can keep them if you want," she said. "They were on my charity pile anyway."

Mrs Stein smiled, "I always thought you two would get on well," and then she turned and went off down the stairs, calling over her shoulder, "Have fun!"

For some reason, Pearl and I burst out laughing. It shouldn't have felt so weird to be laughing at nothing because other people did it all the time. I could hear them, in class, behind me, practically wetting their pants with the giggles until a teacher told them off. But for me it felt weird, because me and Pearl didn't really like each other very much, and when we stopped laughing it was awkward and quiet.

Then Pearl said, "Find the one about the Eskimo." She was pointing at the book. "The girl who had to marry a man who wasn't what she thought."

I turned the pages.

"I used to have nightmares about being trapped and alone, and I was always that girl."

"The Legend of Sedna," I said, finding the right page. "I remember that one too."

We looked at the pictures and Pearl shuddered.

"My scariest one was Pandora's box." I said, flipping the pages to find it. There was a picture of a beautiful jewelled box with demons, fire, snakes and swarms of insects spilling out into the air. "That one gave me nightmares. All that evil flooding the world - I couldn't stand it."

Pearl said, "Pandora's Box is my absolute top favourite because it had the best ending. Look!" She pointed at a little golden butterfly, but I found myself staring at her hand.

Pearl followed my eyes and looked down at her hand too. Her smile gone, she explained, "I was burnt in a fire, but I don't want to talk about it."

"Ouch," I said. I remembered Dad coming home one day and telling us there'd been a fire in his hotel and he lost his suitcase and all his clothes. He wouldn't talk about it either, just said he was lucky to be alive. I guess Pearl was too.

That night in bed, I opened my new book to the story of Pandora's Box.

Once upon a time, everything was dark, and a black bird with black wings laid a golden magical egg. When it broke, Eros the God of Love was born, and the world was filled with light.

The shell from the egg became the earth and the sky. Eros called the sky Uranus, and the earth Gaia, and being the God of Love, he made them fall in love. They had many children and grandchildren, and these became the stars in the sky. The most special of all these grandchildren was called Zeus.

Zeus had two sons - Prometheus and Epimetheus. Epimetheus created the animals and Prometheus made Man in the image of the gods. When Prometheus went to find a gift for Man, he discovered his brother had already given the animals strength, swiftness, flight, teeth, claws and fur, and the only thing left to give was fire.

But fire belonged to the Gods and Zeus was furious. As a punishment, he ordered that Prometheus be chained to a mountain for vultures to peck out his liver every day till eternity, and that Epimetheus was given a box which he was told NEVER to open.

Now Epimetheus was married to Pandora, a beautiful and curious woman, and Zeus knew the box would always be a temptation for her. One day, when Epimetheus was out, Pandora could resist no longer and she peered into the box to see what was there.

Suddenly, from out of the box flew all of the horrors which plague the world today - pain, sickness, envy, greed, war, pestilence and famine. Pandora screamed, trying to close the box, but it was too late. When Epimetheus returned home all of the evils had already escaped. Epimetheus and Pandora sat in sadness and despair, unable to believe how terrible life would be from now on.

Later that night they heard a small voice coming from the box. "Let me out. Please let me out." Curious, they went to the box and lifted the lid ever so slightly. "Please let me out, for I am hope," said a beautiful and small golden butterfly. And so Pandora and Epimetheus released her and she flew out into the world, so that whatever horror or sadness was felt, there would always be hope.

Chapter 25

"I've got a job for you two," said Lily at breakfast the next morning.

I continued to spread strawberry jam on my toast and didn't especially notice the silence until Amy elbowed me in the rib bones. "You!" she said, "You and Pearl."

"Me and Pearl?" I said, shocked. "A job?"

And Pearl said, "What do you want us to do?" looking like she was about to run for the door.

"Later," said Lily, tapping the side of her nose with a finger.

"No, tell us now. I might not want to do it. Or I might be busy," said Pearl, flicking her black gloved hand in the air.

"Yeah," I said. "Me too."

Pearl shot me a suspicious look.

"I mean, we're just soooo busy, aren't we? I think my diary's full," I said.

Pearl laughed. "Oh yes, dahling. I've got an important meeting and Hello Magazine is dropping by for a photo shoot."

Lily said, "Very funny, but you've still got that job."

Bianca moved closer to Pearl and linked arms with her. When breakfast was cleared away, she said, "How long are you going to be?"

"I don't know," said Pearl. "I don't even know what we're supposed to be doing."

"Come and get me when you've finished, yeah?"

"Whatever," said Pearl.

And then Bianca sort of gave me a dirty look, like I was trying to break up their friendship or something. "See you later, BEZZIE," she said to Pearl, and went off holding arms with Scarlet.

Lily unlocked a door next to the big room, and introduced us to the DRAMA cupboard. It was more of a messed up storeroom with mirrors, than a cupboard. A kind of jumbled up walk-in-wardrobe. Pearl would have felt perfectly at home in the muddle, but I hated it.

"Mrs Stein's idea," she said. "She wants to put on a play at the end of term, and this lot needs sorting out first."

"You are joking?" I said.

Lily shook her head. "And if you can manage to get through it without world war three that would be a bonus."

"Why us?"

"She seems to think you two could get along just fine if you had enough time alone together. She said something about being stuck in a lift?" She said it with this twinkly look in her eye, like she was up to something; like this was some fabulous joke at our expense. "Anyway, it's not a big job. I'm sure you'll cope," she laughed.

Not a big job? I looked around. We were stranded between dusty shelves, piles of old clothes and battered cardboard boxes with only a roll of black rubbish bags and a broom, when what we actually needed was a bin lorry. I didn't want to touch a thing.

"What was all that about being stuck in a lift?" I said, after Lily had gone.

"Oh that's one of Mrs Stein's favourite fantasies," said Pearl. "She reckons that anyone can get along with anyone if they know enough about them. And if you're

111

stuck in a lift with someone, you can't get away. You have to get to know each other." Pearl kicked at some of the clothes on the floor. "It's nonsense of course."

I peeped into one of the ancient boxes, hoping it wouldn't fall apart or that something evil wouldn't leap out and grab me, and I must have looked like a scaredy lion.

"It's not all bad," said Pearl. "You get to be a neat freak, and I get to show I'm not a total waste of space. Come on, tell me what to do."

I looked around at the mess. "Okay. One box at a time?"

Together, we lifted down the first box and opened the lid. It was full of hats: berets, flat caps, cowboy hats, crowns, beanies, ladies hats with brims and nets, bonnets, horns, ears and all sorts of other weirdities. And right at the bottom was a crushed and battered, black pointy witch's hat. I pushed out the dents and flattened the brim and put it on my head.

"And black is this year's pink," I said, striking a pose.

"Lovely," said Pearl.

"It reminds me of my nanna," I told Pearl.

"Your nanna was a witch?" she said.

For my twelfth birthday Nanna took me to see WICKED, a proper musical play in the West End of London and it's about the witches in the Wizard of Oz. There's Glinda the Good Witch of the North and Elphaba the OTHER witch, the Wicked Witch of the West but it turns out that she isn't really wicked at all.

Pearl picked out a dark red velvet hat with huge bent feathers sticking out of the back. "And this one is from my granny's Harrods collection!"

"Love it, dahling!" I said, in my utterly sophisticated voice.

"Of course, one didn't actually ever get to meet ones grannies," said Pearl in a posh voice, "but if one did, one is certain they would have worn fabulous head gear like this."

I found a hand mirror and gave it to Pearl. She tucked her curls up into the velvet and pursed her black lips, trying to look glamorous.

"Where are your family now?" I dared to ask.

Pearl shrugged. "Well, I'm supposed to have a dad," she said, still looking at herself in the mirror.

"Supposed to?"

I thought she wasn't going to answer me because she carried on with different hats, posing with each one. And I didn't push it. I'd already gone further than I ever thought I would.

Then she said, "I don't know where he is or if I'll ever see him again. I haven't seen him for nearly two years now. He's kind of, gone missing."

"I don't see my dad either," I said. "But I'm glad. I hope I never see him again." I said.

Pearl looked sad. "You've got a mum though," she said.

"Haven't you?"

"She died. When I was seven," said Pearl, trying on the crown.

"And you've been here ever since?"

"Oh god no! Dad was there then. He took time off work to look after me. My mum always looked after me before that because he worked away from home. We didn't see him every week, you know, like a regular family. So it was weird when he was there. Weird but nice. Sort of. He didn't know what to do with me, if you know what I mean. So he took me ice-skating, bowling and all sorts of stuff like that." She looked down at the floor and her voice went quieter. "But then he met someone else and… well, everything changed."

There were noises outside and Pearl stopped. She put her finger up to her mouth to shush me, then tiptoed to the door and pulled it open, suddenly.

Bianca stood there, totally shocked to be caught out.

"Oh there you are," she said. "I was looking for you."

"Why didn't you just come in?" growled Pearl.

"All right all right, don't have a fit. I didn't want to interrupt your cosy little chat that's all." The word cosy had a sneer and a glance at me attached to it.

"What do you want?" said Pearl.

"Doesn't matter," said Bianca. "Catch you later. BEZZIE." She turned away and strutted off towards the stairs.

Pearl closed the door. "She's so possessive. Out of all of us who are here now, she was the first. Then me. She doesn't like newbies. She's a pain in the backside."

I laughed, because I didn't expect that.

And Pearl grinned. "She's not bad really. She was a good friend when I first came."

"So why are you here?" I dared to ask, not really expecting an answer.

"Dad got married, to Barbara. They hadn't even known each other that long, but almost the day after the wedding he went back to work, leaving her to look after me. She wasn't expecting it. And neither was I."

"That must have been really hard for you," I said. It was hard enough losing someone you loved, but to be thrown into the care of a total stranger must have been awful. "Did you like her, this Barbara?" I asked.

"Like's a bit strong," said Pearl. "I mean, I tried. She tried too. She didn't have a clue though. For example, we went to the city farm and animal rescue because

114

that's what I would have done with Mum. Except that Mum loved animals and Barbara just stood around, worrying about the mud on her shoes and making phone calls. So then we went to Bluewater, because Barbara loved shopping. I hated it. Mum only took me so I could go in the play area, but I was too old when I went with Barbara and it was just deadly boring."

"Nightmare," I said.

"And she used to sulk when Dad went away, and moan because he never had his phone turned on and she could never get in touch with him. And we argued and I actually ran away once, except the truant patrol caught me and took me back. Barbara went totally ape and told Dad he had to come home, change jobs, be a full-time dad and everything, and then they argued too. And well, to cut a very long boring story short, I decided to run away properly; to the seaside and work in a fair. Only I didn't want her to think she'd won, so before I left, when they were asleep, I set fire to some of her stuff and it all went kind of wrong. Oops!" Then she held up her hand for me to see close up. "I didn't get very far."

"That's awful!" I said. "And is that when you came here?"

"No, I had a few foster placements then, because Babs threw us out - I don't blame her - and Dad went missing while I was in hospital."

"Missing?"

"Well he didn't have anywhere to live so they never knew how to contact him and he didn't have a job either. But I couldn't stay in hospital forever so they fostered me out. But nothing lasted very long. I didn't behave very well…" she said, using air quotes again. "And then they packed me up and sent me here one night and I've been here ever since."

115

I had about a hundred thousand questions I wanted to ask, but I didn't know where to start. And anyway, Pearl was back playing with the hats.

She picked them up, one after the other, put them on her head, looked in the mirror and then threw them on the floor. I started to put them in neat piles: ladies, men's, joke hats and a pile destined for the black bin bag. But all the while I was thinking how hard it must have been for Pearl.

And then Pearl said "Why do you always carry that bag around? Wouldn't it be easier to leave it in your room?"

I felt the straps; it was still there. I didn't think about my bag most of the time, except that I wouldn't be dressed without it.

"Isn't it heavy?" said Pearl.

I shook my head. "You get used it."

And then Pearl said, "I'm sorry I wrote on that stone."

I shrugged.

"And thanks for not telling on me."

I felt like a low life then because she had apologised and I hadn't, so I said, "And I'm sorry for taking your pink box." I genuinely regretted taking it.

Pearl nodded. There was a millisecond of awkward silence, and then Pearl said, "She cut up the photos. Babs. The evil one."

"Your step-mum?"

"They were all pictures of my real mum."

I cringed. "Oh my god, I'm really, really sorry. I never thought…"

Pearl said, "I forgive you. We're friends now. Except that, if you ever go into my room again without permission…" Her eyes were cold and serious. "… You WILL regret it." Then she pulled a carrier bag from

116

under the shelf and tipped it cheerfully onto the floor, as if her last sentence had never really been said.

I shivered, hoping she was just really bad at sarcasm, but Pearl was already sifting through the pile of utterly revolting granny dresses, and didn't seem to notice my reaction.

"Unless we're doing a play about old ladies with a love of floral prints, we're in trouble," she said, and started to put the dresses on hangers.

At the bottom of the pile was a strange looking black cloak, with a golden silk lining and yellow and orange flame-like flashes sewn around the bottom. We took it in turns to try it on. Pearl flapped the sides like wings. I swirled round and round, trying to make a swooshing sound as I moved. I had a vision of myself being Elphaba, on stage in front of an audience. "I need a magic wand," I said, looking around the cupboard for something that would do. "Or a spell book," I said, grabbing the battered Costume Loan Register from the shelf next to the door.

"And the hat," said Pearl. "The pointy hat." She tipped the hat box back onto the floor and gave me the witch's hat. She grabbed a pair of red devil horns for herself and put them on her head. And then we lost ourselves in dressing up.

By the time we had finished with the cupboard, it was almost back to its original chaos. My friendship with Pearl, however, was clear as mud.

Dear Lucy,

I'm sorry I haven't written anything for so long. I haven't forgotten you.

Nanna used to say there's something good in everything and everyone. I never thought that could possibly be true before, but there is a girl here I didn't like very much at first. She didn't like me either. But now she is my friend. I don't know how it happened but we seem to get on okay. So Nanna was probably right. She usually was.

Love you,
Ruby x

Chapter 26

When Mrs Stein told everyone about the end of term play, Pearl and I were sitting next to each other. I caught myself clapping and looked at Pearl straight away to see if she was laughing at me. Just because we'd spent a morning in the drama cupboard together didn't mean we were best friends and I half expected to see her nudging Bianca, or calling me a saddo or something. She didn't do any of those things because she was too busy looking just as excited as me.

"What play are we doing?" asked Pearl.

"You're going to write it yourself," said Mrs Stein.

"We're what?" moaned Bianca.

Mrs Stein said, "It's going to be a play about CREATION. How the world was made. Or something else if you like. How something began. It's up to you."

Pearl whispered, "No prizes for guessing where she got that idea."

"…And this is how it's going to work. You'll each write an idea as a story first, then I'll pick one and we'll all work on that to turn it into a play." Mrs Stein had a pile of books on her desk; folk stories, pictures books, an encyclopaedia and several books of fairy tales. "You can use these as inspiration but I want you to come up with something original."

We all stood up to look at the books, except Pearl.

"I love making up stories," she said, already writing.

I picked the first book from the top of the pile, a book called, 'Witches, Wizards and Magical Tales'. I could easily have spent the whole afternoon just reading, imagining stories in my head, but I hated writing them down. Pearl didn't look at any books and when I finally sat down again, she had already written a whole page.

"What on earth are you writing?" I said.

"Something about a phoenix, rising from the ashes," she said.

I was impressed with Pearl's imagination when my own brain seemed to have ground to a stop. I wanted to write something about good and evil, and friends who had started out as enemies discovering they liked each other after all, but all I could think about was green witches and people not being as bad as they looked.

"You need to start writing," said Mrs Stein, tapping her watch.

I wasn't the only one having trouble. "I don't know what to write," said Bianca.

"Put down some ideas," replied Mrs Stein. "It doesn't have to be a complete story at this stage. Just let your imagination take over and write whatever comes into your head. You can organise your thoughts later."

Going to see Wicked was the nicest treat anyone could ever have given me. From the moment the curtain went up and the good witch Glinda arrived in her bubble, I was totally captivated. It was just like the Wizard of Oz only better because it was there in front of me; real people doing real acting and singing and dancing. From the start, you have to stop thinking about the good witch being GOOD and the wicked witch being WICKED, because you realise that Elphaba with her freaky green face and black witchy clothes, is actually the good one after all. She's honest, she cares about things and she stands up for herself. Her appearance doesn't matter; only how nice and clever she really is. It sounds cheesy but it's not. There's flying monkeys, fire breathing dragons and the Emerald City, and at the end when the witches end up more like sisters and have to say goodbye, Nanna and I were actually crying.

I floated home in my own bubble of happiness. It was the most amazing night of my entire life. I knew then that if I didn't grow up to be an actor on a stage I would never be happy.

Nanna said she would pay for me to go to a special acting school if it was what I really wanted, but I knew she didn't have the money. She was just being nice.

And then we got home.

Dad was out and Mum was crying. Nanna told me to get some tissues from the bathroom and there was an open pregnancy testing kit on the shelf above the sink. A used testing stick lay next to it, a blue line in the middle of the result window. I picked up the stick and grabbed a toilet roll, then went through to Mum. Nanna had her arms around her and Mum was crying into Nanna's chest. I handed the toilet roll over and showed Nanna the tell-tale stick. She nodded and pretended to look like she was happy, but her smile was totally fake.

Mrs Stein told everyone to put their pens down and asked if anyone would like to read out their story. In the pin-drop silence that followed, I sat back, relieved not to be the only one with nothing to show.

But then, in a very thin voice, Pearl said, "I will." She stood up. Her hands were shaking, so the paper was wobbling. She took a deep breath and read. "Once upon a time, long long ago, when the whole world had been destroyed, there was nothing left except devastation and ruin. A single little ember cried. 'Help me,' in the dark. 'Shut up,' said the rubble. 'Be quiet,' said the wreckage. 'Enough of your moaning,' said the empty black night. The little ember was ready to give up and die when the ashes suddenly spoke. 'Even a blazing fire has to start with a spark,' they said. 'Do not give up hope.' Just then a great wind blew and the ember burst into life, turning into a beautiful multi-coloured bird. The bird was a phoenix and it looked around at the rubble, the wreckage and the empty black night and stretched out its enormous wings. It flew and it flew all over the world, making everything come alive. It flew until kind and good people were born, and it flew until all the people were happy again. And when it had finished, it settled down to live happily ever after."

I had goose pimples on my arms when Pearl finished, and there was like, this huge nanosecond of silence before anyone made a noise or comment. The connection between Pearl's fire and this story was not wasted on me. And I was half thinking it was a really good story, and half thinking how I would never, not in a million zillion years want to read my story out in front of everyone.

Then Bianca giggled.

I turned round and gave her my foulest glare.

Chapter 27

As far as friends are concerned, I didn't have a great history. After Courtney faded out of my life, there was Shania. I had to sit next to her in science because of the alphabetical seating plan, and for a while we hung around together. But then she made friends with Holly and I caught them talking about my dad in the toilets, because Holly's mum had seen him up town, "drunk as a rat," she said. But they wouldn't say it to my face, so I couldn't defend him and didn't like them after that.

Then there was Brittany, Emily and Daisy, who were in my maths group, and for a while that was okay, except they were REALLY DULL and all they ever wanted to do was go to town and try on free make-up samples and I couldn't be bothered. There were others, but we never got as far as swapping phone numbers so it wasn't like they were real friends. And eventually, there wasn't really anyone left, except for the girls who had music lessons at dinner time or the ones who played netball after school, and none of them had even noticed I was alive.

Out of school, there was Alice Walker. She lived on my road and was two years older than me so we weren't like, BEST friends or anything. But she always said hello and asked me what I was doing, and it was kind of nice to have someone bigger looking out for me. At weekends she went to a theatre school, and I thought she was the luckiest person alive.

After a morning in the drama cupboard with Pearl, I sort of forgot that people didn't like me. I started to think we might have something in common and that we were different from the others. When Pearl read her story, I was the only one who didn't laugh and told her it was really good. She held onto my arm when we went over to dinner and we sat next to each other, on our own table. It felt right. There was Amy and Rachel, Bianca and Scarlet, and Pearl and me. Everyone had a best friend.

And then that evening, Mrs Stein said we'd worked really hard and earned a DVD and popcorn. We all went up to our bedrooms to get our pyjamas and duvets, and I felt all excited and happy about having a proper friend to sit next to; someone to share my popcorn with. I even told Lucy's photo what I was doing and imagined her talking back to me.

But I was last down, and when I got there Pearl was sitting between Bianca and Scarlet on the three-seater, no room for me. Amy and Rachel were on the double with their teddies and there was just one armchair left. A single.

Bianca gave me a smug look and linked arms with Pearl. Pearl didn't seem to think it was a problem to leave me on my own and anyway, she was busy divvying up the popcorn into three bowls. I looked at the armchair. I looked at everyone else sat next to a friend, and I didn't want to be the odd one out any more, so I left.

"Where are you going?" Pearl called after me.

I didn't answer, but I did hear Bianca laughing.

Back in my room, I picked up Lucy's picture. She looked so happy with her hands in the air and a tiny drum on the floor between her little fat legs. Her eyes were huge and her hair was growing, thick and curly like mine would normally be. I hoped she would never remember or know what an epic failure her big sister was, because I would never let her down again.

Chapter 28

There was a noise outside, so I blew my nose, wiped my eyes, and sat against the door.

"Ruby? Are you all right?" said Lily, on the other side.

"Yes," I sniffed.

She tried to open the door. "Can I come in?"

I stood up; catching sight of my tear streaked and snotty face in the mirror before Lily came in.

"Ruby! What's the matter?" she said, arms open wide in a nanna-ish kind of way. I buried my head in her chest and wrapped my arms around her middle, so she couldn't see my face, which was totally lame because she'd already seen enough. "Come on, Luvvy," she said. "Talk to me. I'm a good listener."

Nanna was a GREAT listener and she always made me feel better.

"Are you going to tell me why you've been crying?" said Lily.

I wanted to tell her, but it just sounded so silly.

I told Nanna I was lonely. She stroked my hair and said, "Everyone feels lonely at times, but it won't last. Before you know it, you'll be making new friends, going to new places and having all sorts of fun."

Outside the snow was falling. Kids were dragging sledges past my front gate on their way to the common, chucking snowballs and laughing with each other.

And then Nanna said, "How about an early Christmas present? Will that cheer you up?" She went to her bag without waiting for me to answer, and pulled out a large white envelope. "It's not wrapped, but I've a feeling that won't matter."

I took the envelope, unable to think of a single thing which would cheer me up; after all, friends don't fit in envelopes.

"Come on, Ducky. Open it."

The envelope was new and crisp. I lifted the flap and peered inside. The first thing I saw was money. Twenty-pound notes. Lots of them. Held together with an elastic band.

"Nanna! I can't take this."

"Not the money," she said. "Although you'll need that too. It's the other thing; it's what the money's for."

So I pulled out the clump of notes and with it, a leaflet…

THEATRE COACH
Acting, Singing and Dancing Tuition
Develop your Talent
Increase your Confidence and Have Fun
Musical Theatre Skills taught by Professionals
For 5-18 years

I held the leaflet and the money in my hands and stared. Speechless.

"I want to make your dreams come true," said Nanna. "It's on Saturday mornings at the YMCA buildings. You do a bit of everything. I've already spoken to the lady who runs it. You just have to fill out the application form and take it along with the money."

"But…" The leaflet had pictures of children acting and singing and dancing, doing all the things I dreamed of doing. "This is where Alice Walker goes," I said eventually. And then I looked at the money. I didn't like to count it out note by note, but there must have been two, three or even four hundred pounds there. "Nanna, you can't afford this," I said.

"I've been hiding a bit away every week and I want you to have it. I want you to be happy."

"I can't…"

"You can, silly girl. You were born to do this. Take it. Enjoy it. It's what life is all about."

I squeezed Nanna so hard then that tears came out of her eyes. "I love you, Nanna. Thank you," I said. "It's the bestestest present in the whole wide world." I looked down at the money and the leaflet and tucked them all back into the envelope.

"Now put that somewhere safe," she said. "You don't want to mislay it."

"No way," I said, because it was far too precious a gift to lose. I slipped it behind the bread bin, ready to show Mum when she came home from work, not quite able to believe that my dream really was about to come true.

Lily passed me some tissues. I blew my nose and wiped my eyes.

"Come down and watch the film with us, eh?" said Lily.

"Nobody wants to sit next to me," I mumbled.

"That's not true," said Lily. "Because I want to sit next to you and I'm not nobody."

Nanna and I watched the kids chucking snowballs at each other. It looked like so much fun.

Nanna said. "Let's you and me build a snow-woman."

So we put on coats and gloves and scarves and Nanna put on her hat and we went out the front and played in the snow until all the kids who'd gone up to the common were on their way back. We were cold and wet but we'd made a beautiful snow-woman and just as we were about to go in, Nanna saw Alice Walker with her boyfriend. She nudged me, "Go and tell her you're joining Theatre Coach."

I didn't want to interrupt anything but Nanna was really excited for me, so I did it for her. I told Alice I was starting at Theatre Coach and Alice said it was "cool" and that I could go with her until I got to know people, and then she invited me to a party that night at her boyfriend's house. He was even older than her. I had never been invited to a party before.

And then Alice said "Oh my god!" and she was looking at something behind me.

When I turned round, Nanna was on the ground. I didn't see her fall, but Alice said she'd slipped in the snow. Alice and her boyfriend helped me to take Nanna into the house and I offered to call an ambulance.

Nanna told me to stop clucking like a chicken.

When Alice left, I made Nanna a cup of tea with two sugars and some of her own home made shortbread.

"Are you all right?" I asked. She didn't look very well.

"Don't worry about me. I'm just a daft old bird who can't stand up for falling down," she said.

I phoned Mum to tell her about Nanna's fall, but she was getting ready for the Christmas 'do' at work and up to her eyeballs in vol-au-vents and sausage rolls. Not to mention that she was pregnant and tired. I probably shouldn't have bothered her. She said she'd come home as soon as she could, but not just yet.

Then Nanna told me to go to Alice's party. I wanted to stay in the warm, looking after her. I didn't know anyone going to the party, apart from Alice, and I would have felt like a spare part because Alice had a boyfriend and I didn't, but Nanna insisted.

Sometimes, grown ups get it wrong. They don't mean to, they just don't understand.

"I'm all right," I said to Lily. "Just feeling a bit homesick maybe." I stood up, went over to the window and pressed my face onto the glass.

"Is it so bad staying here?" Lily said.

I shook my head. Nobody knew me. It was best that way. "I'm not a nice person," I said.

"Of course you are," said Lily "Whatever makes you think that?"

I remembered a funny tasting drink. It was supposed to be a raspberry fizz. "Like a slush puppy, only less slushy and more fizzy," said Alice. And one drink became two became three, and then it wasn't a problem that Alice had disappeared because suddenly I could talk to anyone.

"It doesn't matter," I said to Lily. "I think I'll go to bed now."

When Lily left, I felt sick. I hadn't thought about Alice since the night of the party. And I didn't really want to think about her ever again. I tried to write to Lucy…

Dear Lucy,

Nanna and I built a snow-woman. She said women were better than men.

We rolled a big fat round body from the snow in the front garden, and I collected snow from the street to make the head. Nanna gave me her hat and scarf to tie around its neck and then Nanna got some orange peel for the mouth and a carrot for the nose and I found some pretty stones for the eyes. I said it looked like Nanna because it was the prettiest and loveliest snow-woman anyone had ever seen...

But I couldn't write any more. I got changed, brushed my teeth and got into bed, pulling the covers up, practically all the way over my head. And then I screwed up my eyes, held my breath and tried to think about anything other than THAT night. If you keep dead quiet, don't say a word and don't even breathe, no one knows what you know. And then you can just get on with your life again and all the bits that hurt, you just put them in a box in your brain and throw away the key.

Chapter 29

With big black bags and puffy red eyes, I dragged myself out of bed. Splashing water on my ugly face didn't help and it didn't matter that it was the first day of rehearsals for The Phoenix, because there was no way anyone was going to see me like that.

I didn't go down for breakfast, and when Lily came up to see me, I told her I was ill. She offered to get me some toast in my room, but if I was going to do ILL convincingly, I had to refuse. Five minutes later, there was another knock and I got it into my head it was Lily, so I opened the door, head bowed and holding my tummy, hoping to give the impression I was ready to curl up and die.

But there were Pearl's stacked heel boots and I couldn't stop myself looking up.

"OH! MY! GOD!" said Pearl. "Can I come in?"

"No, I'm ill."

"Really?" she said, pushing past me. "You look more tired than ill. Have you been awake ALL night?"

I didn't really need to answer because my eyes welled up and I flopped back onto my bed, utterly exhausted.

"Frankly, Ruby, you look bloody awful!" Pearl got me a box of tissues.

"I'm not coming down like this," I said. "You'll have to do the play without me today."

"No way," said Pearl. "I'm not having Bianca mess it up. You're the only one who understands what this means to me. No one else knows about… you know, this." She held up her gloved hand. "Not even Bianca. I need you." Pearl held my chin, moved my head from side to side and pushed her fingers up through my hair. "God, your face is exactly the same shape as mine. I'll do you a Pearl Special and we can be twins for the day. Nobody will even know."

She left the room, but minutes later came back with armfuls of colour pallets, pencils, bottles, brushes and a scruffy make-up bag from which she pulled out a hair band to lift the fringe off my face. And then she set to work.

When she finished, I was allowed to look in the mirror. The whites of my eyes were still pink, but only if you looked close. Mostly what you saw was green shadow with heavy black lines feathering away across my cheeks, shiny black lips with an extra deep Cupid's bow and white skin. My short hair was gelled into spikes.

Our arrival in school was a PERFECT moment.

To say we caused a reaction was an understatement. Bianca totally hated me and I don't think the others were too delighted by our stunning TWIN effect make-overs.

When we finished our work (as in Maths and English), we had to sit in the big room to talk about the play. Mrs Stein said we didn't need a proper script because it wouldn't be very long, and thought that turning it into a dance would be better. Pearl wasn't very happy and I didn't want to lose out on my chance to act in real play, so we had a vote. The other four all voted for the dance thing, with a narrator. I looked at Pearl, but her face gave nothing away. Without any comment, she stood up and I thought she was doing a runner. But she only went as far as the drama cupboard and returned seconds later with the silk-lined black cloak.

"This is for the phoenix," she announced. "And I don't care what anyone says, Ruby's going to be the phoenix, or we're not doing it."

Bianca said, "You can't say that!"

So I said, "It's Pearl's play. If she wants me to be the star, it's up to her."

Mrs Stein nodded. "And I agree. What does everyone else think?"

When nobody sided with Bianca, she got a right strop on and said she wasn't going to be in it. But Pearl did what Pearl did best; call it manipulatation, flattery or whatever you like, it worked. She told Bianca that she really wanted her to do the set design, what with her being such an artistic genius and everything. Then she convinced Amy that she was the only one who could find some really nice music because she had an iPod. She insisted that Rachel's fashion savvy would make her the only person to choose costumes, and that Scarlet was absolutely the right person to put together the dance moves. As for me, apart from being the phoenix I was also the publicist, responsible for inviting people to be in our audience.

Pearl had everyone eating out of her hand.

My Nanna used to say my dad could "charm birds from the trees," and I thought about that when Pearl was busy organising everyone.

After supper, Pearl came to my room. She was utterly excited about doing the play and inviting guests to watch us. "You will invite my social worker won't you," she said. "I might get into a nice foster family if they think I do good things. No one wants a kid who starts fires."

"You'll get a nice family," I said.

"But you will make sure you write won't you? Big me up. Say something like it's written and directed by me. Maybe we could take some pictures at rehearsals and send them too. What do think?"

"I'll say it's BREATHTAKING, COLOURFUL and MAGICAL."

"Oh, that's amazing," she said. "You're so clever." Then she reached over and hugged me. I'd never had a friend do that before.

Chapter 30

I was more and more convinced that meeting Danielle was a waste of time. Playing games couldn't possibly be doing me any good, especially when everything in my life was improving anyway. So I put on my red converse, arrived late to our next meeting, and told Danielle I was ready to go home.

"You've come a long way, Ruby," she said, and then paused. It looked like she couldn't find the words she wanted to use. "Do you understand what I mean by... closure?"

Of course I understood. "Yeah, End Of. It means there's nothing more to say. And there isn't, so can I stop coming here? Can I go home?"

As usual, she didn't answer me with a straight yes or no. Instead, she went and got some paper, scissors, a glue stick and some coloured pens. Gel pens they were, really nice.

"I've got a little exercise for you." She gave me the black pen and said, "I want you to draw a door, on three different pieces of paper. "Just three plain doors, nothing fancy, but make them nice and big."

I drew three giant rectangles and put a handle shaped line on each of them.

"Now on one door, I want you to write PAST, on another door I want you to write PRESENT, and on the last door I want you to write FUTURE. And then I want you to decorate the doors, or colour them in, or leave them blank. That's up to you. You can use the colours if you want."

I shrugged. It wasn't like, a massive deal or anything and the gel pens were sooo nice to use because the ink flowed onto the paper without you even having to press hard or anything. I started off with rainbow stripes, because they were easy. But I got braver and started to experiment with squiggles and swirls and by the time I finished, the three doors were all covered in groovy patterns with loads and loads of colours. I was quite proud of my art work. And Danielle said they were beautiful.

Next, I had to cut along the top, down one side and across the bottom of each door, so that it opened, and then I had to stick the paper with the opening door onto another piece of paper.

"Now you have three doors. If you were to open each one, you would see something from your past, something about your present and something in your future. In the space behind the door, I want you to draw something from each of those times in your life," instructed Danielle.

"But I don't know what is going to happen in my future," I said.

"That's okay. This is just a bit fun. Draw whatever you want," she said.

I opened the door to my past and sat looking at the space for a while. Lots of thoughts went through my head, but I couldn't decide what to draw. So I opened the door to my present and that was easy. I sketched a picture of a bird; my idea of a phoenix, and coloured it with bright orange and yellow. I drew a huge yellowy sun in the blue sky and green hills all around, with a yellow brick road stretching off into the distance. I made sure to decorate it with pretty little flowers because flowers are easy. Everything was easy, and I didn't want to stop drawing. Then I remembered Mum and Lucy. I couldn't leave them out. And Pearl too, my new best friend. So I carried on drawing and filled up all the space behind the door, and continued around the door too, so that my picture was everywhere, and even if you closed the door, there would still be pictures to see. I used every single gel pen, and every single bit of white paper was covered.

When I finished I showed it to Danielle. She asked me about the bird, and I told her it was the phoenix from the play. I couldn't wait to do the play and dress up and feel like a bird, flying free. Just thinking about it made me grin like an idiot until my cheeks hurt. I don't know what Danielle must have thought.

"Maybe you'd like to draw what you see behind the future door?" suggested Danielle, which was a great idea because it gave me the chance to prove how much I had to look forward to and how I wasn't going to do stupid window crashing stunts ever again.

The first thing I drew was our new house; just a square with a roof, and four windows. I couldn't do it properly because I didn't even know what our new house looked like. I drew me and Mum with her orange hair, and Lucy, all looking out of the windows. But there was one window empty. I wanted to draw Nanna, because that's how I would have liked it to be, but even in pretend, Nanna wasn't going to be there in the future so I couldn't. Instead, I drew Pearl with her black curly hair and black lips and gothy make-up and then I drew some black lips and green eye-shadow on my face too, just like our twin make-overs.

And then I got stuck. It wasn't as easy to look behind the future door and my brain was empty of ideas.

"What else can I draw?" I asked Danielle.

"Anything that comes into your mind," she said. "Whatever you draw is good."

I found myself chewing the end of the black gel pen and when I looked, it had teeth marks, so I stopped chewing and tried to think of something else. I picked up the green pen and drew some grass and a tree, and covered the tree with little blue birds, and then just to fill up the page added a load of random people. They weren't very good. It wasn't nearly as nice as my other picture. "Oh yes, our new house needs a front door." I said, and picked up a red pen to squeeze a door between the two downstairs windows. It was a bit tall and thin and stick-like, and it didn't look right, and I didn't like the way it stood between my window and Pearl's either. "That looks more like a wall than a door," I said.

I bit my nails instead of the gel pens and tried to come up with something else to fill up the white space on the paper, except I couldn't because Nanna should have been there and wouldn't ever be there again.

"Can I do the other door?" I said.

Danielle swapped the door to the future, with the door to the past. With the black pen, I drew Nanna first. I made a really good job of Nanna, doing her silver hair, blue eyes and her lovely smiling face. You can't draw wrinkles. I coloured her clothes all colours too, even though she usually didn't wear bright things. She had her arms open wide and a speech bubble coming out of her mouth. I wrote, "I love you, Ruby" inside.

I looked down at Nanna and didn't know what else to do. There wasn't anything else I wanted to draw. Nanna was just Nanna and nothing else was good enough to be next to her, except maybe some flowers and birds.

Then I was finished. I bit my nails again and looked out the window. There was a flap of skin down the side of my thumb and I chewed at it. I knew it would bleed if I pulled it off and I didn't want to bleed all over my picture of Nanna, but I hated it just hanging there. My front teeth clamped down and ripped the flap free. It didn't even hurt. Blood started to pour down my thumb and I shoved it into my mouth.

Danielle handed me the tissue box and I wrapped a tissue around my bloody thumb instead of sucking it.

"Do you want to draw anything else?" she said.

I closed the door with Nanna and the flowers and birds behind, and I had this horrid thought that I was closing her coffin and quickly opened it again. But it didn't take away the image of her, dead. So I picked up the black pen and started to scribble on the outside of the door. Backwards and forwards, side to side, a proper mess. The paper went soggy and fell apart. It was all ruined. I scrunched the door picture up into a ball, and threw it across the room.

I rewrapped the tissue round my bloody thumb because it was still bleeding, and I squeezed it really hard, because that's what you're meant to do to stop blood. When it dried up, I opened my bag and started to take the stones out, one by one, onto the table.

Danielle went to the tap and poured me a glass of water. "It is really difficult for you to think about your past isn't it?"

I drank the water and didn't take my eyes off the bloodstone and put it in the middle of the table. Nanna said it was really green jasper, dotted with iron oxide to make the drops of blood red. It was supposed to be shiny and reflect the light, except it was dull and smeary, so I took one of Danielle's tissues, breathed onto the stone and polished it till the red was sharp and gleaming again. Then I arranged the other stones into a perfect never ending circle, with the bloodstone in the middle and the fossil outside.

Chapter 31

We all made a list of people to invite to the play - family, social workers, care workers and some of the local people who lived in houses nearby - and Mrs Stein helped me to make the invitations. We stuck another list, a GUEST LIST, on the dining room notice board. New names were added as people accepted their invitations. Pearl was always the first to check it in the morning, and when her social worker's name was not there she had a face like thunder.

And then on Friday morning Lily was handing out letters, and I got one and Amy got one and then, PEARL GOT ONE. I put mine in my bag; it was from Mum. Pearl ripped the envelope apart and pulled out the letter. I held my breath.

"Oh my god oh my god oh my god," she squealed, fanning her face with her hand. "She's coming. And guess what else? She's bringing someone to meet me. Oh my god it might be a FOSTER MUM!"

She ate breakfast with a massively huge grin on her face and every now and again she had to stop and laugh. When she finished breakfast, she went and wrote on the guest list, "Pearl's guest + 1"

While she was writing, I opened my own letter…

Dear Ruby,

An end of term play? I can't wait. We always knew you would be an actor. What is the play about? Is it okay to bring Lucy? She's still teething, but I'll give her something to chew on during your play. I promise she won't spoil it. I can hardly wait to have my two girls together again. I've told Lucy all about it and she keeps saying 'Duby' which must be your name in Lucy speak!

I am going to book us into a B&B overnight so we can spend some time together the next day, if that's all right with you.

We're going to be a family again, Ruby. The house swap is going ahead and you will have a lovely big bedroom when you come home. It will be just us girls. I mean that too. Nanna would be so proud.

All my love,
Mum and Lucy xxx

When High Fell had gone to sleep, I read Mum's letter again. She said, just us girls. She always used to say that when Dad was away, only then she meant me and her, and Nanna of course. It was like, our signal for good times, for girly fun.

Except that it never lasted. I crossed my fingers and hoped it would this time.

Chapter 32

In the big room, everyone was painting scenery. Tom had made two large wooden screens with hinges in the middle, and flame shapes cut into the top. It was Bianca's idea. They were free-standing and on one side we were going to paint orange, yellow, and red fire, and on the other side, trees, green hills and snow covered mountain tops. With the help of a gigantic and disgusting piece of oily garage cloth we would have scenery for the three scenes sorted; a ruined world, a fire, and the beautiful world at the end.

The fire painting was almost finished and Bianca said I should start on the other side. I started to cover the wood in green emulsion, but paint dripped onto the floor and bled through the gaps where the hinges were. Green into orange, red and yellow equals brown.

Yeuch.

Bianca totally freaked. "What do you think you're doing? We've spent all morning working on this, you idiot."

"Shut up!" I said. "It's not my fault."

"Well whose fault was it then?"

Not mine. "I shouldn't even be doing scenery. I never said I was any good at painting. I sent out the invitations, remember?"

But Bianca just kept on and on and wouldn't shut up. I put my hands over my ears and closed my eyes to block her out, and she tried to pull my hands away from my head. Tom came to rescue me and when Bianca stopped shouting, he sent her to time-out.

Pearl said to me, "Why don't we go and listen to the music Amy's got. Tell me what you think. You're about as much use here as a chocolate teapot."

It was the third time she'd used that expression and it jolted me. I looked straight into her unpainted face. It was almost like looking at a ghost.

"What?" she said. "Why are you looking at me like that?"

"My dad used to say that about my nanna."

"I'm sorry," she said. "I didn't mean to…"

I shook my head, not quite believing what I was thinking; that not only did Pearl look a teensy bit like me, she was not a million miles away from looking like my dad.

"Are you all right?" she said. "You've gone all white."

I shivered, had goose pimples on my arm and a strange feeling in my tummy. I followed Pearl into the classroom and watched her put Amy's iPod in the iPod dock, but I couldn't take my eyes off her.

The music was something classical. "Amy had a little help with this," Pearl said, using air quotes. "She said it was weird…" (air quotes again), "…but Mrs Stein is very keen we use it. Do you like it?"

I was too busy looking at Pearl looking like my dad looking like me, to even think about the music. "I don't know," I admitted.

"Look, why the hell do you keep staring at me like that?" said Pearl.

It was her eyes. It could have been the hair, but the hair was obvious and I was used to it. Lots of people have black curly hair. But since her eyes were usually hidden behind dark make-up and spidery lashes, I'd

145

never realised before; they weren't just LIKE Lucy's eyes, they WERE Lucy's eyes.

"You're creeping me out," said Pearl. "And there's still such a lot to do. This is MASSIVELY important to me. My whole future could depend on it."

It wasn't a good time to talk. "Sorry," I said. "Can we start the music again? I wasn't listening properly."

Pearl put the music back to the start. I tried to listen. It sounded like film music, but apart from that I still didn't have an opinion. When it finished, Pearl said, "I absolutely love it. It's perfect. It's even called The Firebird. It's Mrs Stein's idea really, but we'll let Amy take the credit. Oh I could listen to this over and over…" And then the iPod froze or something because the music stopped, and Pearl said, "Damn!" and started fiddling with it. She only stopped when she noticed me still staring at her.

"Sorry," I said, looking away. "It's just that we look so alike…"

"Oh don't go on about it. Before I came here people were always saying doesn't she look like her daddy. It REALLY wound me up. I've just got a common kind of face. So can you stop acting like some kind of mad stalker and get on with making this play brilliant?"

Chapter 33

The house was dark and totally quiet and I should have been asleep for hours, except that I couldn't sleep. My brain was all over the place, darting around, sifting through the past few weeks and everything I knew about Pearl.

The baby photos and how like me and Lucy she was.

The way we looked now.

The way we could both eat anything and stay stick-thin, like my dad.

Our part-time dads.

And then the book; 'THE WORLD OF CREATION STORY BOOK', which wasn't just a book, it was my book, with Nanna's shopping list inside.

And then I thought, I am crazy. Pearl was right. I'm completely off my trolley. How could Dad have had another daughter without us knowing? It's just bonkers.

But the idea wouldn't leave me alone. I couldn't even get into bed because my legs had a major case of the twitches. And staying still was impossible. I tried lying down and felt sick. I tried pacing up and down my room, but felt dizzy, and in the end I settled for sitting cross-legged on my bed, staring at Lucy's photo trying to find an answer. "Just because we've all got the same hair and the same eyes, it doesn't make us related," I said. "Lots of people have curly hair…"

I picked up the 'The World of Creation Story Book' and opened the pages. I touched the words with my fingers, smelled the pages and held the shopping list in my hand. "Even if it is mine," I said, "Doesn't mean a thing. It could have gone in a charity bag. Nanna was very keen on recycling old things. And Pearl's dad might have found it in Save the Children, or Oxfam or something…"

My tummy ached. I felt sick. I stood up, grabbed my bag of stones and tipped them onto the bed as softly as I could so they wouldn't make a noise. I started to arrange the stones in a square pattern, with a big square on the outside and smaller squares inside, but every time I moved, the mattress dipped and the stones rolled out of their straight lines, knocking against each other. I picked up the fossil and examined the shell pattern imprinted into the rock.

"What do I do?" For all the years it had been on this earth, it didn't have an answer. So I picked up the other stones one by one, examining every solid inch of their little hard bodies. "Talk to me," I begged.

Back when I was little, my lovely purple amethyst would have told me what to do, not with words, but with feelings. Just holding it would have been enough to help me think straight. When I got to the bloodstone, dusty again and uninspiring, it sat there blankly.

"Talking to myself and seeing things which can't possibly be true?" I said. "I am definitely going mad."

Chapter 34

The morning of the play, I didn't want to get out of my bed. It was warm, the sheets were soft and cosy and my body felt too heavy to move. Outside my room, I could hear the others all fussing like cowardly lions and moaning about how they were scared of looking silly and getting laughed at.

But to be honest, I was nervous too. Not just because it was my first ever public performance and every one would be looking at me, but because I was embarrassed about what I'd been thinking and what Pearl must have thought of me. "Noooo, I can't do it," I groaned, pulling the covers over my head and wishing I could go back to sleep.

But it wasn't to be. Someone banged on my door.

"Go away," I said.

"Come on, Luvvy. Time to get up. Can't lie there all day," said Lily.

"Please don't make me. I don't want to be here any more."

Lily opened the door and popped her head round. "Don't go all prima donna on us today, Missy." She winked. "This is your big day."

"It's Pearl's big day," I said. "I'll probably ruin it."

"But you're the star of the show." Lily pulled my curtains and opened the window, letting the summer air do its worst. I did my top sulk and then hauled myself out of bed, dragged some clothes over my unwilling skeleton and lugged it downstairs.

While I stuffed four slices of toast and jam into my face, Tom sat next to me and started banging on about the need to work as a team and help each other with all the preparations. The big room needed tidying, the floor sweeping and the chairs setting out... Boring boring boring.

When we thought everything was ready, Mrs Stein said we had to fold the programmes and put one on each chair. It wasn't a big job really. I mean, there were probably only about 30 people coming to watch us and it should have taken ten minutes tops, but Pearl didn't like the way we were doing them.

"Make sure you get the folds really neat with a good crease," she said.

"Hello?" said Bianca, all offended. "I think I do know how to fold."

Then Pearl told Amy and Rachel, "Put one on each chair, right in the centre so it looks tidy. Don't just throw them on." And to Scarlet she said, "Staple any spares to the notice board, but do it nicely, like a proper display..."

Bianca said, "You are SUCH a bossy cow."

And Scarlet agreed. "Yeah, where do you get off, telling us what to do?"

Then Pearl suddenly flipped. "Getting it right might not matter to you, but it matters to me," she squealed. "My WHOLE FUTURE depends on this play."

We all looked at her for a minute. I wondered if she was going to cry. But then Bianca said, "Don't be a drama queen! No one gives a damn about us. They'll all come and watch us prance around like idiots, clap a bit, have tea and then go home."

"Yeah, without us," added Scarlet.

"Even your old man has given up on..."

She never got a chance to finish. Pearl turned on Bianca, swinging her right arm round and punching her hard in the jaw. Bianca screamed and grabbed her face. You could tell it hurt because she just stood there howling and didn't even bother to fight back. But Scarlet wasn't going to let Pearl win and pushed her backwards into the wooden screens. The screens and Pearl fell over, and Scarlet sat on top of Pearl brandishing the big stapler and shouting, "If you don't shut your bossy mouth I'll use this on it!"

Pearl squirmed to free herself. I watched; my hands and arms twitching, ready to help Pearl. She looked at me with big eyes, just like my dad used to look at me when Nanna was telling him off. "Get her off me," said Pearl.

And I nearly did, except I wasn't quick enough and Pearl managed to roll Scarlet onto the floor without my help.

"Thanks for nothing!" she shouted at me, finding her feet.

Just as I was about to protest, Mrs Stein appeared out of nowhere. "WHAT DO YOU THINK YOU'RE DOING?"

Bianca was still bawling like a cry baby, Amy and Rachel scuttled behind Mrs Stein, and Pearl and Scarlet stopped killing each other.

"I'M WAITING FOR AN ANSWER."

Bianca let go of her jaw. It was already developing a purple bruise. "She hit me," said Bianca through sobs, pointing at Pearl.

"She said my dad didn't care about me," said Pearl.

"He doesn't…" said Scarlet.

"THAT'S ENOUGH!" said Mrs Stein. "Amy, go and get Tom. The rest of you, sit down. Away from each other."

We all found a chair. I sat near Pearl at the front. Bianca and Scarlet went to sit at the back of the room. Pearl sneered. "Some friend you are."

I looked at the scenery we'd spent so long painting. Even after my disastrous help it still looked beautiful, except that now one of the hinges had broken. Tom arrived and picked the screens up. We had to sit in silence for twenty minutes while he mended the hinge and made sure we didn't move, or speak, or kick off again. I kept looking at the clock, thinking about Mum and Lucy arriving and us all being there in disgrace and not being allowed to see them.

When Mrs Stein returned, she gave Tom the keys to the minibus and said there were visitors waiting at the station and they needed collecting. She said, the play would go ahead and prattled on about consequences, and nerves getting in the way, and she made us apologise to each other. We all said the words; I doubt anybody really meant it. And then we had to tidy up the mess while we waited for the visitors to arrive.

Pearl grabbed a broom and swept the floor. She kept looking out the window. "I hate this place," she hissed. "I cannot wait to get out of here."

Chapter 35

Mum had Lucy on her lap in the front row. Lucy looked so pretty in a little white smock with embroidered yellow flowers, and she was chewing insanely on Mum's purse. I was literally desperate to give her a hug, but knew I had to wait till after the show. Mum was wearing a navy skirt suit and silky blouse, so she looked smart, but not like she was going to work. She was holding a tissue under Lucy's chin so the dribbles wouldn't spoil her dress. When Mum looked up, I waved and she guided Lucy's little hand to wave at me. Lucy was all bright eyes and smiles, but Mum smiled with her mouth only.

I must have looked nervous. I definitely felt nervous. Rocks crashed into each other in the pit of my stomach and I felt sick.

Pearl waited across the room, scanning the audience, but she wouldn't look at me. She was ready to start the music, but just before she did I saw her smile and wave discreetly. I followed her line of sight into the audience, hoping to see her new mum, but there was just one person waving back. I gathered she was Pearl's social worker. Alone. And she sat down next to Amy's creepy scar-face of a dad.

Everyone got into position, and the music started.

It was hollow and eerie, with a sad horn telling the destruction of Pearl's world. Bianca was narrator. "Once upon a time, long long ago, when the world and the entire universe had been destroyed by evil, there was nothing left except devastation and ruin, and a single ember…"

My nerves disappeared. A violin started to play a sweet tune. I was no longer Ruby Garnett. A little ember was coming to life, and I reached up into the air, feeling around the empty world with my bare hands. Scarlet and Amy danced around me. (They were supposed to be the rubble and the wreckage and not nearly as important as the phoenix, but Amy kept getting in front of me and I had to resist the temptation to stick out my foot and trip her up.) A trumpet, and then lots of violins joined in, getting louder; then a recorder or a flute, and a big swelling up of drums beating and I could practically FEEL the phoenix coming to life; beating her big strong wings and flying off around the world, happy to be alive. Scarlet was the warmth of the sun, driving away all the bad things. I stood up, rising from the ashes and flapped my multi-coloured cloak around like the wings of a phoenix bird, and I was in another place. The music lifted me up, freed me, and I left everything else behind in another world.

Bianca said, "The beautiful bird flew and it flew until new lands were made in the shadow of its beauty. It flew and it flew and new people were born, good people, happy people. It flew and it flew, creating a new world. And when it had done, it settled down to live happily ever after."

When the clapping stopped, Mrs Stein stood up and gave a speech about our hard work and told everyone how proud she was of every single one of us, and how Pearl had not only written the play, but directed it too. Pearl had to come out and give a special bow and she got another clap from the audience.

Swept up in the moment I went to hug Pearl. "Awesome," I said, meaning her, the play, me and everything.

But Pearl was rigid, like hugging a tree trunk. "She was supposed to be here," she said, staring past me into space.

"Don't get upset. Don't let it spoil your day. It's been brilliant."

She looked at me then, straight in the eyes and said, "What is the point in being brilliant if no one cares?"

And then she walked out.

I wanted to go after her, but ached to see Mum and Lucy too. I was torn.

The audience were standing up and the other girls had gone to talk to their visitors. Pearl's social worker was looking at her watch and I don't think she even noticed Pearl had gone. Lily announced that there would be tea and buns in the dining room. I looked at Mum and Lucy, now standing, moving sideways towards the door. I chose my family.

Lucy kicked her legs and I took her from Mum; a moment I had been dreaming about for too long. She was chunkier, cuddlier than I remembered. I kissed her soft baby cheeks and held her little fat hand. "I'm sorry, Luce," I whispered into ear. It felt so good, so right, to be together again.

Mum half-smiled at me. She looked really down and miserable to be honest; not what I was expecting after my first ever REAL performance. No "Encore!" like there used to be.

"Is everything okay?" I asked.

Mum shrugged. "I need to talk to Mrs Stein," she said. "Will you come and find me when you're changed?" Mum took Lucy from me.

"Has something happened?" Dad's turned up. She hates the play. She hates me. "What's wrong?"

But she didn't want to talk to me.

Chapter 36

I changed my clothes as fast as was humanly possible and rushed back to find Mum. She was in the lounge, waiting for me with all the other visitors. Mum was talking to Mrs Stein. She was carrying Lucy on her hip and sort of rocking and jigging from side to side. I couldn't see her face because she had her back towards me, but Mrs Stein looked all serious and was totally fixated on whatever Mum was saying. Until she saw me. And then Mrs Stein suddenly put her hand up to stop Mum from speaking, and in an utterly fake gushing way, said "And HERE she is, our little STAR."

Mum turned round. Her nose and eyes were red. "Darling!" she said.

"When have you EVER called me Darling? What's wrong?"

There was a quick look between Mum and Mrs Stein; if you'd have blinked you would have missed it. But Mum used to do the same with Nanna, and my lie radar was well tuned.

"Shall I go and find your little sister a biscuit?" Mrs Stein said to me. "Doesn't she look like you?" And in a second, they were off to the land of milk and cookies.

Mum took my hand between hers.

"TELL ME," I demanded. "It's Dad isn't it? He's back."

"Not here," she said. She led us away through the mob of social workers and broken families to Mrs Stein's empty office, and we both sat down on the sofa, facing each other. Mum dabbed at her nose with a tissue then took a deep breath.

She fixed my eyes with hers and said, "He ISN'T coming back."

"Then what?"

"I have some news," she said. "It's not good news, I'm afraid."

But Dad NOT coming back was good news, to me at least. "What do you mean?" Mum looked down. I could see her searching for words.

"Well?"

Mum looked up and stared into my eyes. There were tears in hers. "The police are looking for him," she said.

"What's he stolen this time?" I said, even though I didn't want to know.

"Stolen?"

Mum's talent for ignoring the obvious never failed to amaze me. How you could be married to someone for fifteen years and not even notice they were thieving was just mind-boggling.

"Doesn't matter," I said, no time for confessions. "Why are they looking for him?"

You could see her, wrestling with the words, not quite knowing how to break it to me, whatever it was. When she did speak, her voice had dipped to a whisper and she was speaking into her chest. Something about getting married. But I couldn't quite hear her.

"What are you saying?"

Mum took a deep breath, sat up straight and blurted it out. "Your father is wanted by the police because he has another wife…"

"But he's married to you! I've seen pictures …"

"I know, Baby. But the police are looking for him because he also married someone else, before he

158

married me. It's called bigamy. And it means he's never really, legally been my husband."

There was a clock on the wall. It said ten past four.

About an hour later, it still said ten past four. Time stopped. The world exploded into a zillion tiny pieces. I tried to piece them together again, but I knew life would never be the same again. Those things I was thinking, about Pearl, and me, and sisters; they might be true. "But it was JUST a wife, wasn't it?" I said, desperately trying to cling on to the last fragments of another world. "I mean, he didn't have other kids, did he?"

"Oh, Baby, I never even thought of that." Mum's hands reached up to shield her eyes, her face. When she pulled them away, she looked twenty years older. She shook her head. "I honestly don't know." But then almost immediately, added, "No. No, he couldn't have. He wouldn't have. No, I'm sure he didn't."

It's called denial; where you insist something is one way, when on some other level, you KNOW it isn't. Mum was an expert at it, and until that moment, so was I.

"He used false names. That's how he got away with it… Ryan Garnett isn't his real name," continued Mum.

But all I could think was, PEARL IS MY SISTER.

Chapter 37

Just then, I hated my dad more than I hated anyone in the whole wide world. I hoped the police found him, arrested him and sent him to prison. I didn't ever want to see him again, but I was scared Mum would.

"What are you thinking?" Mum asked.

"I can't begin to tell you," I said, standing up.

Mum shook her head. "Whatever you're thinking is fine. I know this is a shock and I understand how you feel."

I doubted very much that ANYONE would understand what I felt, because as much as I hated him, he was MY dad, the only dad I had. He screwed up, messed up and ruined everyone's lives, which I had grown to accept, but now I discover that he didn't just do that to me and Mum and Lucy, he was doing it to another family. Or maybe more? Who knew what he was capable of?

And then I had a thought. "If he's not Ryan Garnett, who am I?"

"You're still Ruby Garnett," said Mum. "That doesn't change. It's your legal name and it always will be. And you're still my daughter. You're still his daughter."

But it was too much. I put my hands up to my head and closed my eyes. Why was everything so impossibly difficult? "I'm sorry," I said. "I need to be on my own."

Mum nodded, and I left her sitting all alone on the sofa, crying real tears.

Chapter 38

Pearl was in the lounge having an ANIMATED discussion with her social worker. "I don't give a rat's backside about second thoughts…" she screamed.

Flesh and blood, I thought, staring at her.

Everyone else had scattered into the garden or the kitchen or some other place and I don't imagine for one minute this was accidental.

"And you can get lost too," she said, turning on me. "With friends like you, who needs enemies?"

I wondered only very briefly about announcing my news. Hey Pearl, don't worry about your foster family because you've got real family after all. I'm your half sister, we share a dad; oh and by the way he's a bigamist. I didn't even know, one hundred percent, if it was true; the sister bit that is. It never occurred to me to doubt Mum about the rest of it.

In my room, I emptied my backpack onto the floor, picked out the bloodstone and held it between my hands, up close to my face. "Help me," I whispered, because my brain was filling up too quickly with thoughts about Pearl, and Lucy, and how in the world we would manage to live our lives knowing that we were sisters.

But I needed proof, rock solid proof.

Chapter 39

There were two signs on Pearl's door. One said DO NOT ENTER – OR ELSE. The other was a programme for The Phoenix Play, written and directed by Pearl Jasper.

I opened the door. Pearl's mascara smudged tissues were strewn across the bed and make-up spilled out on the chest of drawers in front of the mirror. The pink box was there too, and I picked it up and opened the lid. The torn photos had been stuck together with tape. I flicked through them looking for a photo of my dad I might have missed the first time, but there were none. I didn't have much time.

My eyes darted everywhere while my hands pulled open her drawers and rummaged in her clothes; same again with the wardrobe and the suitcase on top. A canvas bag full of gloves hung from her mirror so I looked in there too. I didn't have much time.

There was still one place I hadn't looked; under the bed. On my hands and knees, I felt all along the darkened floor. I could actually feel the soft fluffy layers of dust, but didn't dare to look in case I breathed in toxic filth and died of some horrendous disease… and then suddenly, the biscuit tin.

Of course! Why else would anyone keep a rusty old biscuit tin under their bed, other than to fill it with sentimental rubbish you didn't want on display? I pulled it out and sat with it for a moment. I had the weirdest goosebumps down my back, and my hands felt strangely limp. My eyes screwed tight shut because I was almost too afraid to look. "It might be biscuits," I said, but my fingers tingled and my body trembled. "And if it's not, will I like what I find?" What's the point of truth anyway, I wondered. I could just walk away now and everything would be normal. Ish. As normal as life could ever be when your dad is a bigamist.

Outside the door, I heard a movement.

My heart raced.

This could all end so badly. Getting caught red-handed in Pearl's room was like having a death wish. There was only enough time to stand up before the door burst open.

"Ruby? What the…" said Pearl, eyes ablaze and practically spitting blood.

"Please don't hurt me," I said. "I just had to see you."

"You're in my room," she said. "And I warned you…" and suddenly she was on top of me again, lashing out randomly with her fists. We fell onto the floor, fists flying, and the pair of us rolling around. Pearl hit my head and my shoulders, and I tried to stop her, to hold her whirling arms just long enough to speak, but she was raging. I don't know how long she beat me. It didn't hurt and I didn't scream or cry…

In the end, she ran out of fight and collapsed on top of me in a big soggy heap. Her tears wet my cheeks, and my arms wrapped around her sobbing, jerky body. We were connected. Flesh and blood. I couldn't deny it any more.

"It's all right," I said. "It's going to be all right."

Pearl rolled off me, and onto the floor. Looking up at the ceiling she said, "Nobody wants me, Ruby. Nobody wants to meet me. Nobody wants to find out who I really am. Nobody gives a damn. As far as they're concerned, I'm just a thirteen-year-old fire raiser with anger issues and black finger nails." She sat up and looked at me. "And not one single person in the whole world cares…"

Her eyes said nothing. All I could see was a dark emptiness. The fire had gone.

"I care," I said.

Those empty eyes looked straight through me.

After a few seconds, I said, "Pearl, what's in that biscuit tin?"

"What?"

It must have sounded insane and insensitive. "I'm sorry, I just wondered… I mean… I was in here because… because…"

"A stupid stone," she said, flat and all out of fight. "It was supposed to make my dreams come true."

"A stone?" I repeated. "What kind of stone?"

"Have a look. You'll probably like it knowing you. It was a present from my dad. He said it was pretty, and I was pretty…"

I felt goosebumps on my arms and down my back, and my eyes flicked towards the tin, then back at Pearl. Not just once, but several times.

"What?" she said.

"Is it … is it …. Purple?" I said.

Pearl gasped. "How do you …?" And before she finished the sentence, she grabbed the tin and prized off the lid.

"My amethyst!" I cried.

"Yours?" said Pearl.

But I couldn't answer. I sat there with my mouth open, staring at the most precious stone of all. I dared to pick it up, gently, scared. And as my finger tips felt the magic crystal, I knew it was the most completely beautiful thing I had ever seen. The proof I needed was staring back at me, calling my name. I looked up at Pearl.

You could almost hear her thinking, two and two makes four.

"Explain," she said.

"My things used to go missing on a regular basis," I said. "Things I loved; this stone, the book of creation stories, other books and toys. I never knew why they disappeared or where they went. At least two of those things are in your room, now. Gifts from your dad."

"What are you trying to say?" said Pearl, her forehead creased with frown lines.

"Dad," I squeaked, barely able to hear myself and I didn't think Pearl had heard.

But she said, "My dad?"

I tried to find the right words. "No... our dad."

Chapter 40

"Our dad?" she said, eventually.

Water filled up my eyes, and I couldn't stop staring at Pearl, watching, waiting for her to react. Neither of us moved. I think I held my breath. Pearl's face was blank.

"I think we have the same dad," I said eventually, desperate for some reaction. "And I think he was married to both our mums at the same time."

Pearl let out a deep breath and then said something I didn't expect; not even from her. "Jesus, Ruby. You are one sick joker. How could you say that?"

"It's no joke," I said, shaking my head, never taking my eyes off her.

"But it's a stupid idea. It's not true. My dad was Frank Jasper. Your dad was somebody or other Garnett. It's crazy."

She was right; it was the craziest thing. How could it have happened that we were there, Ruby Garnett and Pearl Jasper, in the same school at the same time and we just happened to be related? It was too much of a coincidence and even I doubted it was true at that moment. But then I looked back into Pearl's eyes and they were my eyes, Lucy's eyes, my dad's eyes.

Pearl grabbed my chin, and moved my face from side to side. Surely she could see the likeness, the genetics. And the amethyst; she knew it was mine.

"But how do you know?" said Pearl. "How do you know for sure?"

"Apart from how we look?" I said.

Pearl nodded.

"That," I looked at the purple rock. "And the chocolate teapot thing, back on that walk to the meadow; you sent shivers down my spine. And then, I don't know, just seeing your face without make-up, his disappearing acts, the way you are, that we both lived a stone's throw apart, the fire…"

"The fire?" said Pearl.

"My dad worked away a lot too, and he came home once with all his stuff burned. He said he'd been in a fire…"

Pearl looked down at her hand and pulled off her glove. We both looked at the scars on her hand and then she nodded. She was beginning to believe it too.

"There were just so many little things. I was desperate to tell you, but I didn't have any proof. And then today, Mum told me the police were looking for him. He's been using different identities. He's a bigamist and they want to find him."

"Are you serious?" said Pearl. "Does anyone else know? About us, I mean."

"I'm totally serious," I said. "And no one knows about us. I came in here to find proof. I'm really sorry. I should have talked to you, but I didn't want to say anything if it wasn't true. I'll never ever come into your room again without your permission."

Pearl shook her head. "I don't know what to say, what to think… What does it mean?"

"Oh Pearl, don't you see? It means you're my sister. We're family."

Pearl covered her mouth with her hands, like she had to stop herself from speaking, but her eyes were still smiling and filling up with tears at the same time. I reached over and gave her a hug and we sat there like that for I don't know how long. All the time I was thinking how Nanna used to say that good things could come out of bad, and at the same time I was hoping, really hoping, that this was a good thing.

Chapter 41

Outside, I heard Lily and Mum, and Lucy squealing. Pearl and I let go of each other and Pearl wiped her eyes. We heard Mum open my bedroom door across the hall and say, "She's not in here…" Then footsteps, the bathroom door and, "She's not in here either."

Lucy squealed some more.

Then Mum: "Where's Ruby?"

Then Lily: "Let's ask Pearl."

Then the door handle.

I looked at door, looked at the amethyst and Pearl and back at the door. "I'm not ready to tell anyone else," I said, shoving the amethyst back into the tin.

I grabbed the lid at the same time as Pearl, and somehow it flipped from our hands, upside down onto the floor. And there, crudely sellotaped to the inside of that lid, was a photo of Dad.

Pearl's door flew open.

Mum's smile turned instantly to a look of horror and she gasped, almost dropping Lucy. She didn't even look at me. Her eyes were huge and round and staring. I followed her line of sight to the upturned biscuit tin lid.

No one breathed, no one moved.

All eyes were on Mum.

Eventually she said, "What's HE doing there?" her voice was shaky and I thought she was going to cry.

We looked at Pearl, waiting for her to speak. When she didn't say anything, I said, "There's something you should know."

But Mum was ahead of me, and staring at Pearl. "His hair… his … curls… his eyes."

Lucy started to cry. It broke the spell and I jumped up. "Sit down," I said to Mum, guiding her to Pearl's bed. I picked up Lucy and sat down next to Mum. The three of us looked down at Pearl.

Lily had barely moved and I don't think she had any idea what was going on. But the penny dropped when Mum said, "So that two timing low-life had kids after all…"

Pearl's lips started to wobble.

"Mum, it's not Pearl's fault…" I started to say.

But she was too upset to listen.

Chapter 42

Mum was in a totally mental state of shock and not actually able to do anything more than beg fags off the kitchen staff and stand outside chain smoking. Tom had taken charge of Lucy, and Lily took Pearl and me into the staffroom away from the others, who got DVDs and popcorn in the lounge as a bribe not to kick off. Mrs Stein arranged for Mum and Lucy to stay over in the guest bedroom.

Pearl and I talked about Dad. She kept saying, "I can't believe it," after every story we swapped.

And even though it was true, I wasn't sure I did either.

"What are we going to do?" she said. "I mean, what happens if he comes back and takes me home? Won't it be weird?"

She still believed in him? She still thought, after all this time, and wanted by the police that he would turn up and be a proper dad again? "He's not coming back," I said.

She went totally still, staring straight through me, at nothing. I could almost see her brain working, trying to piece together the fragments of her life. "But if he never ever comes back... what will happen to me?"

"You can live with me," I said. "We're family, remember." I didn't think it through. It was just one of those things that sneaks out of your mouth before you have a chance to object.

"Do you mean that?" said Pearl. "I mean, do you really really mean it?" There were tears in her eyes and a smile hovering, waiting to burst through.

How could I say no? So I said, "Of course I do," and the moment I said it I was glad. Glad because Pearl wasn't just my sister, she was my best friend.

Chapter 43

Mum was in the kitchen drinking coffee. She had at least calmed down a little. I told Pearl to wait outside while I talked to Mum.

I went in and gave Mum a hug. She looked like she needed it.

"Pearl's nice," I said. "And you know it's not her fault."

"Yes," said Mum. "But people say and do things they don't mean when they're upset."

I said. "Yeah, you told me already."

"I'll apologise," said Mum.

I looked at her. Wondering what she'd think of my request; knowing full well that she might say no. But Mum wasn't a bad person. She was Nanna's daughter. She had a heart. "Mum?" I said. "Pearl doesn't have anyone else."

"It's very sad," said Mum. "I wonder how many other lives he's ruined."

I could see Pearl, through the glass strip, listening. "But it doesn't have to end like this," I said. "I mean, Pearl needs somewhere to live. I've got a big bedroom, you said so…"

Mum closed her eyes and counted to ten. "No," she said. "Absolutely not. You don't know what you're asking. It will never work. I'm sorry, Ruby."

"Please? She's on her own..." I glanced at the door, but Pearl had already gone. "Mum!" I said. "She needs us…"

But Mum was shaking. "NO!" she snapped. She pulled a crumpled pack of cigarettes from her bag and went towards the door. "I am not discussing it. Ever."

I stood there for a second, or maybe a minute. Nanna would never have put Pearl in that position and I missed her so much it hurt.

And then I went to find Pearl, except that she didn't want to talk to me either.

I wanted to scream, or shout or break a window or throw a rock or… anything to get rid of this impossible situation. I couldn't see a way out.

Chapter 44

When bedtime finally arrived, I was glad. Glad to be on my own. Glad not to have to talk or try to be understanding or take sides.

I flopped on my bed and listened to the oral hygiene police outside my door. They had the good sense to leave my teeth to rot, so I put my pyjamas on and climbed into bed waiting for the noise to die. When they all finally shut up, I pulled up the covers and closed my eyes.

But too much had happened in a day and my head was full of pictures. Memories dripped in; a leaky tap you couldn't turn off. It started with the play, Mum, Lucy, Mum's news about Dad, Pearl screaming at her social worker, Pearl's room, the amethyst, Pearl's face, Mum's face... then him. His eyes, his smile, his dimples, and the last time I ever saw him...

Alice Walker left me at the gate and went away laughing with her new boyfriend. I went up the garden path; the snow-woman was still there although she was starting to melt. There was a notice in front of her, written in my dad's drunken scrawl. It said "I'll be dead by the morning." His idea of a joke. My heart sank. I wasn't expecting him to be home and he was the last person I wanted to see. I would never have left Nanna and him alone together, especially when Nanna didn't feel well.

I had a house key, except that I couldn't quite find the hole in the middle of the lock, no matter how hard I tried. "Shhhh..." I kept saying to myself, "Must not wake Nanna."

And then the door opened.

"Well well well! Had a little drinky did we?" he laughed, glass in hand and barely able to stand up.

And there was I, in a spinny world that wouldn't stay in focus, and I laughed too because suddenly it was the funniest thing that had ever happened.

We stumbled into the kitchen and Dad got me a shot glass. "Just a night cap," he said, filling it with brown stuff. "For my pretty, pretty Ruby..."

I saw the bread bin then, pulled away from its usual place, and the wall space behind it was empty. "Where's my money?" I garbled.

"Come on, Ruby, we're celebrating!" said Dad.

I took the shot glass because he gave it to me and I wasn't thinking. I couldn't think. All I knew was that my money and my Theatre Coach application form wasn't there. "Have you got my money?" I said.

And then there was Nanna in the doorway, holding on to the door frame. "Put that drink down, Ruby!"

"Fun sucking kill joy you are, Lucinda," slurred Dad

"You. Go to bed," Nanna ordered me.

"She's already had a packet! One more won't make any difference." Dad hiccupped.

"He's got my money," I said.

And then the floor started to wobble, and I felt very sick.

"Up. Stairs. NOW!" Nanna said, in her no messing voice.

So I rushed out of the kitchen and up the stairs and I tried really hard to get to the bathroom, but there were more stairs than I remembered and the floor was moving away from me and I just couldn't hold it any more …

…Fizzy pink cocktails spewed up all over the landing carpet.

"A chip off the old block…" laughed my dad, at the bottom of the stairs.

Together, they picked me out of the pile of puke and took me into the bathroom where I sat hugging the toilet basin. Nanna told Dad to clean up and he refused; said it was woman's work. They argued. They called each other names and their voices got louder and louder until I couldn't stand the noise. I reached back to slam the door shut, but it was too far and I fell over.

My eyes squeezed tight shut to stop the room from spinning.

Nanna demanded my money back and Dad laughed. He said it was a pipe dream and that Nanna was throwing her money away. I wanted to stand up and object. But another wave of sick came rushing up my throat and out onto the floor where my face was.

Dad laughed. "Chip off the old block," he said, again.

And Nanna screamed, "Get out!"

"Pleasure," he said, and went off stomping down the stairs, swearing at Nanna and banging the front door behind him.

I lifted my head out of its pool of vomit and saw Nanna. She said something, I don't know what, and she put her hands up to her head and then just fell over, backwards. No warning. No reason. Just thud… thud… thud… down the stairs.

She called out.

I lifted my head; my hair stuck with sicky glue to my face. "Nanna?" I cried. "I'm coming. I'm coming,"

177

because I would always be there for Nanna. I promised her. "Nanna, hold on!" I shouted.

Somehow I stood up and went to the stairs. A bucket of water sat next to my half-sponged vomit on the top. Down at the bottom, Nanna was twisted and awkward with blood on her head. Lying, crying, moaning, calling my name.

I gripped the banisters and went to her as fast as I could, one step at a time. And when I reached the bottom, I knelt down by her side and cradled her bloody head, pressing the bleed, trying to stop the flow.

I said, "I'll phone an ambulance, Nanna. Everything will be all right."

And then she went quiet. And still. Dead still.

The silence was scarier than anything. I wanted Nanna to be cross with me, and tuck me into bed and make everything all right.

But she never did.

She was never cross, and she never tucked me into bed again.

And then the world started spinning again, but I held her hand, so that she would know someone was there, and I stayed there until Mum came home.

It's my fault she died. She told me not to drink. She told me how bad it was and I knew she was right. And I should never have gone to the party and I should never have drunk the red fizzy stuff, and I should never ever have left her.

I thought about my dad then; his black curls and big eyes, his craziness, his drunkenness and wondered how in the world he could marry more than one person....

The night of Nanna's accident was the last time I saw him. He stole my money and my dream then left me, drunk and incapable. He left Nanna when she was ill. He left Mum, when she had a baby due. He didn't care about anything, and I never wanted to see him again. I didn't want him to know Pearl and I had met, and how for the briefest time, we had been best friends.

And that's when then I realised I couldn't take no for an answer. It didn't matter what Mum thought or how weird everything had become, Pearl and Lucy and me would always be sisters. We had a blood bond and nothing would ever change that.

Chapter 45

I slipped a hoody over my pyjamas and pulled my red converse onto my feet, then opened the door really quietly. Out in the hall, I could hear the night staff in the kitchen, and the creaking of the building as it cooled down. Cold air was blowing up the stairs.

At Pearl's door I stopped. I had to talk to her even if she didn't want to talk to me. I would ask her to give Mum time to get used to the idea. I knew she'd come round in the end. I was shivering and there were goose pimples on my arms and legs. I knocked, very gently, and pressed my ear to the door.

Nothing. No movement, no answer.

I knocked again, louder, but I didn't want to wake anyone else up.

"Pearl," I whispered, knocking at the same time. "Pearl!"

When she still didn't reply, I turned the handle. It squeaked and my heart was in my mouth. I was expecting to see Pearl lying in her bed, sobbing quietly about how the world had let her down and how her life was over.

But still nothing happened, so I pushed open the door and went in. The light from the hallway lit a small area of carpet, but Pearl's bed was in darkness. I went to close the door and my foot kicked something in the way; the under-the-bed tin. It was still open, and empty. The photo of Dad had been ripped from the lid and torn into a hundred pieces on the floor. The amethyst was gone.

"Pearl, it's me, Ruby," I whispered in the dark, resisting the urge to get onto my hands and knees and look for my beautiful rock. "Your sister."

Pearl didn't move.

"Pearl," I repeated louder. "Please wake up, I want to talk. I've got an idea." But still she didn't move. "Pearl, Mum's shocked and upset. She loses it sometimes, but she always calms down and I know she likes you." I moved closer and closer to her. "Pearl, I can't bear to lose you. We're family now."

If I was Pearl and Pearl was me, I would have said something. I wouldn't have been so stand-offish. I wouldn't have left me alone in the dark trying desperately to be friends giving nothing back. "Please talk to me Pearl," I said. And then one last try. "We're sisters. We should stick together." I reached out then, unable to stop myself. I wanted to be close to Pearl. I needed to be close to her. And I put my hand on her shoulder…

Except it wasn't her shoulder, it was her pillow!

"What the…?"

I pulled the covers back, to find two pillows! I had been baring my soul to a sack of feathers.

But if Pearl wasn't in bed, where was she?

I rushed back into the hall and checked the bathroom. I knew she must have run away. It was so typically Pearl to go off on one like some poor deserted drama queen… but she didn't have to. She had me now. So I went back into my room, grabbed another jumper and my bag, and then ran down the stairs two at a time, no thought for keeping quiet now. The narrow window next to the front door was open and the door was bolted shut. I slid the chain and slipped the bolts then rattled

181

the handle, but knew from experience it wouldn't budge. "If Pearl can squeeze through..." I said, pulling myself onto the narrow window sill. "So can I."

Lily appeared in the hallway, with Tammy behind her. "Ruby! What are you doing? Get back in here!"

"Pearl's done a runner and I'm going to find her," I said, jumping onto the concrete step outside.

Lily came to the window and shouted after me as I ran down the path, but there was no way she'd get through it. She would have to go and find the keys. She could shout all she wanted. I wasn't listening.

Chapter 46

There was enough moonlight to see where I was going, and at the end of the drive I looked left and right. Pearl was well gone and I could only guess which way she went. To the left, the road went uphill; to the right, it went down. I started to run downhill, down the lane and round the bend, arriving at the stile into Fellside Meadow. If it was me I'd keep off the road away from cars. So I climbed over the stile and stumbled across the field, tripping on the bumps, dips and stones.

I stopped to catch my breath. "Pearl!" I shouted, and stood silently straining my ears for an answer. "PEARL, WHERE ARE YOU?" I could hear the wish of the night wind in the trees, but no Pearl, so I started to move again.

At the stream, I jumped on stepping stones. It was the exact same spot where I'd seen the kingfisher. I looked downstream and remembered Mrs Stein's warning about the waterfall. Only now in the dark did I wonder where it was, but getting wet was the least of my problems so I carried on tripping and stumbling into the woods, calling Pearl's name. The woods were thick and the moonlight could not reach through the heavy tree tops. It was darker and blacker than ever. Spooky noises made me stop and listen; an owl hooting, strange squeaking and clicking, and a rustling of leaves which could have been anything from a werewolf to a crazy mad axe murderer. "Think!" I said, out loud trying to sound brave and courageous, but my weak and shaky voice wouldn't have fooled anyone.

I remembered Pearl laughing about running away to be near the sea and getting a job in the fair, and suddenly I had this vision of Pearl skipping off down the road to Morecambe Bay. Like a light bulb turning on in my brain, I knew that's where she would be heading. It was SO obvious. And the more I thought about it, the more pictures there were in my head; pictures of Pearl riding the waltzers, stuffing her face with candy floss and ice cream, building sandcastles and wearing silly pink umbrella hats. So I turned round and tried to retrace my steps through the woods to the road.

Except as soon as I turned round nothing looked the same, and the more I looked the more confusing it got. Trees are impossible to tell apart in the dark, and a path didn't exist. I started to walk in the direction of where I came from, but within a few steps I bumped into a large fallen tree lying right across my way. Unless someone had sneaked in, chopped it down when I wasn't looking (silently) and covered it in years of moss and creepers, I was going the wrong way. Without a doubt, I was lost.

In a wood.

On my own.

In the middle of the night…

And no one knew where I was. My only choice was to wait till morning, or continue to bumble blindly about in the dark.

I sat on the tree trunk and took off my bag. Of all the USEFUL things I could have put in it, rocks and stones from my stupid and miserable life were surely the most completely and utterly POINTLESS. I took out the other jumper and wrapped it over my shoulders, and then I heard the rustling noise again and the sound of a dog barking in the distance. I looked around, but couldn't see anything.

Don't be a total baby, I thought. There's nothing here that can hurt you. Crazy mad axe murderers do not stroll around random woods in the middle of the night looking for victims. "And werewolves do not exist," I said, out loud.

And then I heard something else, a whiny high pitched squeak. It could have been a bird, or a rat, or anything. I was shivering and hungry, and knew that if I stayed on that tree stump I would probably have wasted away by morning. So I stood up and forced myself to keep walking.

When I heard the stream again, I started to run, because in school they taught us that streams and rivers always flowed towards the sea. If I could follow that stream, I would find the sea. And if I could find the sea, I might find Pearl. And if I could find Pearl, everything would be all right. It was my little glimmer of hope, in a dark dark night.

Chapter 47

I sang as I followed the stream, feeling lighter and quicker.

"Somewhere, up on a hilltop, eyes are blue. And her black curly hair should have given me a clue…"

I knew where I was going and flew from one bank to another, over branches and rocks. Nothing mattered any more except finding Pearl. The woods started to thin out and every now and again I caught sight of the night sky, full of stars and promises.

"Somewhere up on a hilltop, I'll find Pearl. She's the sister I dreamed of, not just another girl…"

We had our whole lives ahead of us to look forward to, and I sang louder and louder, calling to Pearl between verses, wishing she would answer.

The stream narrowed and the rushing water got louder as it squeezed into less space. Jumping across was easy at first, but the landings were more and more rocky and dangerous and I had to stop before every leap and talk myself into it. Some of the rocks were wet. Slipping into the gushing water was the last thing I needed.

I stopped to catch my breath, and above the noise of my heart beating and the water roaring I heard that high pitched squeak again, except that now it was less of a squeak and more of a voice.

"PEARL?" I shouted, hoping.

And then I heard her. "RUBY!"

My whole body trembled. "Pearl, where are you?"

"I'm over here," she shouted back, her voice very shaky. "Go and get help."

"No! I'm coming to get you!" I called, trying to sound like I knew what to do. "Keep talking so I can hear where you are!"

"No!" shouted Pearl. "There's a waterfall!"

"I know! But I don't care!"

There was a complete break in the trees. I could see the starry sky and Morecambe Bay stretched out before me.

"And it's steep…" she said.

The hill dropped without warning and I started to slip on the loose stones. I tried to hold on to a branch, but it had prickles and they cut into my hands and I had to let go. I fell on my bum. Pearl screamed my name, but it was too late to answer. I went tumbling down the hill on a scree slide, head over heels over head over heels …

Until THUD!

A tree broke my fall. My arm took the shock and I heard a crack before my body wrapped itself around the trunk. I couldn't breathe. For a minute there was total silence. Then I heard the gush of water, and I managed to gasp in a lungful of air.

"Ruby? Are you okay?" called Pearl. She was either shivering or crying. "I'm over here," she said. "By the waterfall."

My eyes opened. Moonlight shone on the waterfall's silvery sparkle as it rushed over the stones to a pool at the bottom. Pearl was next to the pool, her leg at a strange angle, and her face screwed up in agony.

I scrambled to my feet, using only my good arm; holding the other up next to my chest. It hurt like hell when I moved. A few yards away, Pearl was half lying, half propped up against a boulder. She had an extra bend above her knee, and I felt sick looking at it. Her leg was obviously broken. Pearl's face was ghostly white and her teeth were chattering.

"You silly cow," she said, "You were supposed to get help, not throw yourself down here with me."

I couldn't actually tell if she was angry or not.

"I'm sorry," I said.

"What for?"

"For not getting help."

And then we both started laughing. It was like being back in school in the drama cupboard, or ganging up on Lily, just being with a friend. Except that now she was my sister.

"How can you laugh with a leg like that?" I said.

"It doesn't hurt," she said.

"Liar." I draped my jumper across her legs, then took off my hoody and wrapped it around her shoulders. It wasn't a cold night and her shivering scared me, but short of stripping off and giving her my own pyjamas, there wasn't anything more I could do to warm her. I looked around for a brainwave. "I'll get some leaves or something. Make you a nest," I said. "You need to be warm."

"I've got a bag somewhere," said Pearl. "I don't know where it is. It's got food and clothes in it."

"So you really were running away without me?"

She nodded. "Do you hate me?"

"Only sometimes," I joked.

Pearl pulled a sorry face and I shrugged it off. We had our lives ahead of us and no one would keep us apart, but right then and there I needed to get Pearl some help and we needed to be safe and warm.

"Does your mum hate me?" said Pearl.

My eyes started to well up. "Look, nobody hates you. Mum liked you before she knew about Dad... she'll get over it. I promise."

Pearl nodded, and winced at the same time. "Do you think we'll ever see him again?" she said.

I bit my lip. I didn't know how Pearl felt. "Do you want to?" I said.

Pearl thought for a moment and then shook her head. "Not really. Not yet anyway. Maybe one day." She reached out and we held hands, looking up at the sky. But her shivering got worse and I needed to get help.

"Where's your bag?" I said. "You need more clothes on and something to eat, and then we can make a plan to get out of here."

"Ruby, it's got the amethyst in it. I was only keeping it to remind me of you. You and your crazy bag of rocks. When I got to the waterfall, I threw the bag down. I was going to climb after it, but something gave way. That's how I fell. I don't know where it is now."

There were two ways down; the scree way and the direct drop. Pearl must have fallen straight onto the rocks. I shuddered, because I knew only too well that she was lucky to be alive. I stood up and started looking around for her bag. It couldn't have gone far. I really didn't care about the amethyst, I was worried about Pearl.

"But where's your bag?" said Pearl, suddenly. "You're not wearing it!"

I had to think twice before I remembered. "I've left it up there," I said, gesturing vaguely towards the top of the hill with my good arm. "Next to an old tree. I'll never find it now."

Pearl pulled a sad face. "I'm sorry; it's my fault isn't it?"

But it really didn't matter any more. Stones didn't matter. Nothing mattered except getting Pearl, my sister, to safety.

Just then, the sound of a dog barking came out from the trees. I stopped looking for Pearl's bag and squinted into the darkness. There were voices too, and then lights, getting nearer every second. And then a man with a torch on his helmet and a rope draped across his chest.

"Over here!" he shouted.

Tom was close behind him, and before we knew it, a whole army of search and rescue people were wrapping blankets around us and making everything right.

Chapter 48

Mum and I were in the x-ray department when we started talking. Pearl was in a ward because it was pretty obvious she had a broken leg and needed an operation to set it straight. Lily was with her. Lucy was being looked after at High Fell Hall.

"I'm sorry," I said. "I just couldn't let Pearl run away, could I?"

"Do you really want her to come and live with us?" said Mum.

"I know it's a weird situation," I said. "And I'm not totally one hundred percent sure about it, but Pearl doesn't have anyone else..."

Mum looked as sad as I felt.

"... Except Dad," I said. "And we both know what that means. If no one fosters her, she'll be living at High Fell forever. Can't we at least, think about letting her live with us?"

Mum faced me. She didn't answer straight away. She must have known how much it meant to me. "Ruby, it's such a BIG step," she said finally. "I'll need time to think it through. I don't even know if we'd be allowed..."

"But you can ask. Can't you? Please?"

A radiologist came out and told Mum we needed to go back to casualty to get fixed up. We walked down a blue corridor to the waiting area, in silence.

"How about we compromise?" said Mum, when we sat down. "We ask if Pearl can come and stay for the

191

holidays. If it works, and we all get on, we'll ask about fostering."

But I wanted her to live with us, and ached to offer Pearl a permanent home. Surely Mum could see that?

"It's worth remembering that she might not like living with us," said Mum. "It would be a huge change for her too. And this way, everyone gets a chance to try it out. If Pearl doesn't feel totally happy then it's not going to work anyway."

What she said felt right. It was true. Best friends do fall out and sisters argue. I didn't believe it would happen to us, but Mum was only trying to do what was best.

"Okay," I said. "A holiday. Just for starters. Yes?" Agreeing with Mum felt nice.

I kissed her on the cheek, but the movement knocked my arm and I winced. Just then a nurse summoned us into a cubicle where a doctor was waiting. He said the x-rays showed I had a small fracture in my radius, which is a bone in the lower arm; in other words, a broken arm. It wasn't bad but I did need a pot to help it set. He sent us down another blue corridor where we sat on an empty row of chairs, waiting for the plaster nurse.

"I need to tell you about Nanna," said Mum, while we waited. "And it's important you listen."

I was through with running away, so I sat there, holding Mum's hand, trying to be brave and yet scared about what she would say.

"She had an aneurysm," said Mum. "It's like a little balloon in a blood vessel which was pressing on her brain. It made Nanna lose her balance and that's why she had those falls. When she fell, the last time, the balloon burst. It could have happened anytime."

Mum had tried to tell me this before but I wouldn't listen.

"It wasn't… your… fault."

My eyes pricked with tears. It was such a relief to know the truth, but it didn't take away the sadness I felt about losing Nanna. I just wished I could have told her one last time, how much I loved her.

When my arm plaster was set, we went to see Pearl. Mum talked to Lily while Pearl and I had five minutes on our own. She had a drip going into her arm with painkillers in, and a metal brace on her leg. She said it was traction, to keep the bits of broken bone apart until they were ready to operate. She looked tired and fed up. I wanted to give her some good news, but held back in case Lily said she couldn't come to stay. But then Mum came over and asked Pearl herself. I looked at Lily and Lily nodded.

Pearl half-smiled, and didn't say anything. I guess it was a lot to take in.

"Do you want to then?" I said, eventually.

"Are you serious?" she said.

"One hundred percent," I said.

And then she smiled properly; a big, yes-please-and-thank-you kind of smile, and my heart beat with happiness.

We were all tired. Lily said we should go back to High Fell. Pearl needed to rest a bit before her operation and anyway Mum wanted to be with Lucy, in case she woke up in a strange place. I wanted to be with Lucy too.

We were in the taxi going back to High Fell when I finally plucked up the courage to tell Mum about Dad, and how he got me to steal Nanna's money. Mum was very upset, and angry, though not with me. She said she would have done the same thing in my place. Dad had that kind of personality where you would have done

193

anything to please him. She knew Nanna had an issue with missing money, but she'd always put it down to her absentmindedness. She was angry with Dad for making me betray Nanna, and angry with herself for not knowing.

"But you couldn't have known," I said.

"I've been a terrible mother," she said,

I held her hand. "And I've been a terrible daughter," I said.

"But I've been more terrible than you," she laughed.

"No way! I am by far the terriblest…"

After everything we had been through, we still knew how to laugh.

Dear Nanna,

I saw a bluebird. It was the most beautiful bird I have ever seen and I thought about how you would have loved it. I think about you a lot. You are with me when the birds sing, when the honeysuckle blooms, and when the strawberries are ripe. Every time I see a rainbow, I feel your joy.

I remember you telling me that something good comes out of everything, and lately I've been trying really hard to concentrate on finding that thing.

For a while I thought it was being able to help Mum when Lucy was born because it made us close. Then I thought it was being in a play; you know more than anyone how much that meant to me. And then I thought it was discovering that Pearl was my sister. How many people end up being related to their best friend?

But maybe it's all of those things.

Or maybe it was seeing that kingfisher; a symbol of peace and inner calm you said. I hope that's true.

I hope life can be how it always used to be when I was with you; safe and happy. You really were a wonderful Nanna. I was lucky to have you in my life, and I will never forget you.

All my love, forever,
Ruby xxx

THE END

Acknowledgements

I am indebted to my friends and family
for their help, feedback, inspiration and ideas
while writing and editing this book.

Thanks to my dad;
the first person ever to read my work.

Thanks to my mum;
who taught me to love words

And thanks to the children who inspired
Where Bluebirds Fly.

.

BRING ME SUNSHINE

(Short-listed for the Mslexia Children's Novel Competition 2012)

Daisy's dad forgets to get dressed sometimes. Little brother Sam hates being told what to do. And Daisy feels more like a parent than a thirteen year-old girl. There's no time for homework, no time for friends, and even worse, she is not allowed to play the drums any more.

And then Dylan Bell moves back into town; a glimmer of sunshine in Daisy's gloomy existence. There's something really cute about Dylan these days, and it's great he's learned the guitar and wants them to be in a band together; but how is Daisy going to find the time?

Bring Me Sunshine is an inspirational story about following your heart, never giving up and living in the moment.

For more information about Wendy and her books, please visit
www.wendystorer.ws

Lightning Source UK Ltd.
Milton Keynes UK
UKOW03f1848050514

231149UK00002B/6/P